EDDIE

Eddie

Renegades Roadhouse Series

K. L. STEPHENS

CONTENTS

COPYRIGHT

Copyright (c) 2023 K. L. Stephens

This is a work of fiction, Names, characters, places, and incidents either are the product of the author's imagination or are used fictitiously. Any resemblance to actual persons, living or dead, events or locales is entirely coincidental.

All rights reserved: No part of this book may be reproduced or used in any manner without written permission of the copyright owner except for the use of quotations in a book review.

Printed in the United States of America

First E-Book published: 2023

Cover Photos Supplied by: Shutterstock

It's Not His Child
But That Isn't Going to Stop Him From Marrying
the Love of His Life

Eddie has waited ten years to ask Anna to marry him. Many of those years were spent in Afghanistan serving in the Marines. The demons from what he witnessed keep him up at night. He feared that Anna would hate him if she knew about the things he did for his country, but when he sees his friends find peace in the love of their wives. He goes home intent on asking for her hand, not getting the answer he was expecting.

Anna stayed true to Eddie all these years, up until about three months ago. Teased about not ever having a boyfriend she goes out with the hometown bully. In that one night her world is turned upside down. Now Eddie is here asking her to marry him, but she refuses to drag him down in her condition. She just has to find a way to tell her parents about the baby.

| one |

Eddie

It's been ten years since I have seen Anna Groves, the last time I was at her house, I felt confident in my brand-new cammies, just back from basic and advanced training, and I was being shipped to Afghanistan in a week. I joined the Marines just after my eighteenth birthday six months before. I wanted to see Anna one time before I left. The door opened before I could raise my hand to knock, her father standing there, "Sir." I nodded to him, then unconsciously moved into an at-ease position.

He looked me up and down, "Eddie." He addressed me, "I see you are back from your training."

"Yes, Sir." I acknowledged, then proceeded. "May I see Anna?" His eyes widened, then he nodded. Anna was only sixteen, too young to get married, but I have thought of nothing but her since a year ago when I saw her for the woman she would be. I have known Anna nearly from the day she was born, our mothers are best friends. Growing up I ignored her as a younger annoying sister until that day. It was instantaneous, I was in love, and that feeling has never wavered.

"Anna! You have a visitor!" Her father bellowed over his shoulder.

I heard her as she bounced down the stairs, appearing at the front door, with a smile on her face, "Eddie!" Surprised to see me, she rushed forward, holding me at arm's length as her eyes roamed over me, head to toe. "You look so handsome in your uniform!" Glancing over her shoulder, her father was scowling at me, I only hoped he didn't notice my growing erection at that the sight of his daughter. Anna turned her head, "Daddy! Don't frown so. We will stay here on the porch." Anna patted her father's arm as she spoke, then stepped out of the door, she motioned for me towards the swing that hung from the ceiling. Thankfully she had not noticed the bulge in my pants, that was not why I was here. Moving over to the swing that hung to the side, just like most houses in this small southern town, everyone had a porch swing hanging on their front porches.

I held the swing still motioning for her to sit first, before I sat beside her, leaving a space between us. The curtains moved in the front window, and I knew her father was watching us. I caught the movement of the curtains after he stepped back inside the house. Smiling at Anna, I leaned a little closer to her and whispered. "Your father is watching us."

Her eyes darted to the window, "He thinks you are going to whisk me away." She whispered back.

Lowering my eyes, I whispered. "Not quite yet." Then I looked at her, she didn't quite understand my meaning, but again I wasn't here to say what I have wanted to tell her for years. But I did have something to ask, and I needed to get it out before chickening out, "Anna, I am being deployed to Afghanistan in a few days."

Her eyes widened in shock then fear, instinctively she reached out and grabbed my hand, "It is so dangerous there." A tear slipped from her eye.

Reaching out my other hand, "No tears." I gently whipped the tear away, "Anna," I stopped, the words almost came out, but I could not say them, she was still too young. Instead, I pulled a piece of paper from my cammie shirt pocket, "This is my APO address. Will you write to me while I am away?" I handed her the paper, "I won't always be around a computer, but my email address is there for you too."

She looked down at the paper and took it. "Yes, I will write to you." There were still tears brimming in her eyes when she looked at me. "Eddie, promise me you will come home safe."

Managing a small smile, "I will try my best." We both knew the dangers of going to that part of the world. Standing, she embraced me in a hug, and I turned my head into the crock of her neck inhaling the scent of her shampoo, it will have to do for now. When I got into my father's truck, I watched her for a moment memorizing the way she looked, sitting back down and looking at the piece of paper, and I saw her wipe away a tear.

Driving away, this was for the best, I had said everything I wanted to say, well almost, but she was still so young. Even though I was just a couple of years older than her, I would feel like an old man robbing the cradle if I said and did the things I longed to do. That was not fair to her, she had her whole life ahead of her, and if I came home in a box, she would only think of me as a friend she knew and lost then could get on with her life. Somewhere in the back of my mind, this thought justified not telling her how I truly feel.

That was ten years ago, so much happened in the years since that day when I last saw Anna. The things I saw in Afghanistan were unnerving, with so much death and destruction. Anna's letters and emails were the only things that kept me sane and going forward. It was her face I saw in the darkness and loneliest times. Even when I closed my eyes at night I could inhale and still smell her shampoo.

But I had friends, Hunter and Conner, who were like big brothers to me, always watching over me. Conner was our Lieutenant and stayed beside Hunter and me when we were injured during one insurgent attack, talking until we were evacuated out of the area. Fortunately, neither of us was seriously hurt, but others in our platoon were not so lucky. My parents came to see me when I had volunteered to escort one of the fallen back to his family, rather than traveling back home.

Serving our country was a family tradition, and I still felt it was my duty to serve so I stayed in for several years. With each skirmish, every member of our team we lost, changed me, and I wondered if I was worthy enough to be with Anna. Finally, one night, Conner, Hunter, and I decided we all had seen enough and planned on leaving the Marines. Conner was the first to leave, then Hunter and I followed him as our contracts with our government ended. Conner bought a bar and dance club in a small town from an uncle, contacting and asking us to come and help with the bar he renamed Renegades Roadhouse. It sounded wonderful, and I jumped at the offer, but Anna was still there in the back of my mind.

| **two** |

Anna

Ten years, since I last saw Eddie. I was sitting in the breakroom of the little store I worked at, looking down at a picture of Eddie on my phone. He took one after he was injured, showing off the scar on his chest. It nearly crushed me when I found out that he had been injured, not knowing how badly he was hurt. In this instance, it was a blessing that his mother and mine had been best friends since they were girls. So, the day his mother called to tell her how relieved they were that he was going to make it through. I stood back from the kitchen door listening, tears of relief fell from my eyes, *he is alive.*

I looked up to see my father when he caught me listening. All I could do was lower my head, as he walked past me. But instead of saying something about me eavesdropping, he just patted my shoulder, then leaned down and kissed my head.

Linda came in plopping down in the chair beside me,

jolting me out of my thoughts. But before I could close my screen she looked over at the picture of Eddie, "Wow, he's hot!" Grinning. "Please tell me he is your cousin that you want to introduce me to."

"No," I answered closing the screen and putting my phone back in my pocket.

Eyeing me, "Is that the guy you have been pining away for years?"

Blushing I stood to go and start my shift, "I have not been pining for Eddie." I had hoped that was the last of the conversation. But it wasn't. For weeks she would ask about Eddie and our relationship.

"He was in the Marines for several years, now he is out," I explained.

"So, ya'll haven't you know..." Linda didn't finish just nudged my shoulder and wiggled her eyebrows.

"NO! Eddie is a gentleman." I blushed.

"That's disappointing. Was going to ask if he had a big dick." She grinned wide.

"I would not know." I was embarrassed and getting irritated by her questions.

"Well then it is time to move on," she announced, with a nod. I ignored her statement but thought that maybe she was right, and I have been pining away for Eddie for all these years. I'm twenty-six years old. Still living with my parents, and no boyfriend, ever. Even opting to go to my senior prom with a group of friends instead of accepting the few offers I received.

"Maybe I should," I whispered under my breath. Linda didn't hear me, she was busy helping a customer, and I was thankful. I would never hear the end of it if she had heard me. There was one problem, I was still in love with Eddie. I probably need to get over him first. My days progressed as normal until one afternoon Billy Yates walked in. Billy didn't walk into an area, he strutted, and much to my surprise and dismay his eyes were fixed on me.

"Billy." I was polite, "Can I help you find something?" There was a smile on my face that I knew didn't reach my eyes. I worked in a woman's clothing boutique, and I couldn't imagine Billy wanting anything in this store.

He ran his finger down the length of my arm, making my skin crawl, "I think I found what I want right here." He smiled. Billy Yates pursued me in high school, but I always turned him down. His family was rich, and he knew it, and used it to his advantage with all the girls in school, promising them expensive dates. The only problem was he wanted payment for those dates, in the form of sex. And boasted about it time and time again. From what I heard; he had not changed since.

I tried to keep a smile on my face as I stepped back from him. "Billy, were you looking for something maybe for your mother?" I gestured to the area; I knew his mother purchased several items.

He scoffed, "No," looking over his shoulder he saw Linda smiling in his direction. Grinning as he turned, "Maybe some other time," mumbling over his shoulder. He moved to Linda, and did the same to her, running his finger down her arm. I watched in amazement as Linda happily gave him her phone so he could punch in his number. Shaking my head, *I am going to have to warn her about him.* I thought, getting back to steaming the creases out of some new garments on the rack.

Hoping that Billy would just move on to another girl as he did in high school leaving me alone, but he didn't. Week after week, he kept coming back, always when Linda was not working asking me out every time. Several times, he even showed up on my doorstep, those days I hated the fact that we lived in such a small town, and everyone knew everyone. My resolve was wearing thin, but I knew if I said yes, to his offer, what he would want in return.

| three |

Eddie

Here I am standing back on Anna's porch, just as I was ten years ago, as the years passed her letters became fewer, and even though I was still in love with her, I just figured she had grown up, and I was just a memory. But I had to find out for certain. I knew she still lived with her parents. Like déjà Vu, her father opened the door before I could knock. "Sir," I acknowledged him.

Again, he looked me up and down noticing the differences in my appearance from the last time I was here ten years ago. No longer wearing a uniform, I was in a pair of jeans and a tight-fitting t-shirt. My hair was still short, I liked it that way and now I had a short, trimmed beard. I was more muscular than ten years ago. He could not see the tattoo I acquired or the scar from the bullet that went into my side, but I could tell he could see the difference in my eyes, of the atrocities I had witnessed and lived through.

Nodding, "Edward. I am happy to see you safe." He spoke. "Your mother has been keeping my wife informed about how you were fairing."

Smiling, nobody called me by my given name, not even my parents. But I assumed he felt that 'Eddie' was a boy's name, and a boy no longer stood in front of him. Stepping back, he opened the front door, motioning for me to come in. I shook my head as I asked, "Mr. Groves, may I please see Anna?"

"Of course." He stepped into the house leaving the door open, and instead of bellowing for his daughter, he went in and found her.

Fingering the engagement ring in my front pocket as I waited for Anna when she appeared she was older, and, if possible, more beautiful than before. As she smiled, she exclaimed. "Eddie!" She stepped forward and wrapped me in a hug. "You're home!" I wrapped my arms around her and pulled her closer to me. I could feel her body tremble as she cried on my shoulder.

"Hush, no tears. I am safe and home," I whispered into her ear, not understanding the real reason for her sobs. Her father appeared, I looked up not releasing Anna, "Mr. Groves with your permission I would like to take Anna for a drive. I will have her home before midnight."

"Of course, you two go on," He replied and stepped into the house softly closing the door behind him.

Not waiting for Anna to say anything, I took her hand and led her down to where I had parked my truck on the street. I opened the passenger door and helped her in. I walked around, climbing into the driver's side, I started the truck. As I drove, I was getting worried; Anna was staring out the passenger window but had not said a word the entire time we drove out to the lake park. When I finally stopped and put the truck in park, she opened the door and slid out walking towards the lake. Her arms wrapped around herself as if she were cold. I grabbed my jacket as I got out, walking up behind her covering her with it, then wrapping my arms around her.

"Anna, are you not happy to see me?" I asked afraid of the answer.

"Oh, Eddie. I am incredibly happy to see you." She uttered. "It's just." Her voice trailed off. Then she surprised me and asked. "Are you going to ask me to marry you?"

Moving my head to the side of her neck, "I was planning to." I whispered against her skin.

Abruptly she pulled away from me saying. "I can't marry you." She held my jacket tight around her, and I could hear her sobs again as she walked further away.

Three strides were all it took me to catch up with her, she was mumbling and sobbing so hard I could not understand a word she was saying. Pulling her to a nearby picnic table I sat her down and then straddled the bench facing her. "Tell me why not," I insisted softly.

Her head was lowered, and she was shaking it so hard, she looked like the teenager I left all those years ago. Finally, she whispered, "I'm so ashamed." Then with a calming breath, she looked up at me, "I am pregnant, Eddie. And unmarried." She sobbed again, "I should have waited for you. Now everything is a mess."

I finally understood. "Who's the father?" I asked, but she just shook her head again, she was not going to tell me.

"You don't know him." She muttered, that was doubtful I thought. I probably knew everyone in this town if not the county if I didn't my parents did. She was too upset to pressure her for an answer, so, I let it drop.

She finally said more to the universe than to me, "I won't get rid of this baby." She laid her hands protectively on her stomach.

A second revelation came to mind, "Did he suggest you do that?" There was a harsh tone to my voice as I asked.

Not even sure she was aware I was still there, she nodded. "What am I going to do?" Anna uttered to the wind.

I stood and then knelt in front of her, pulling the ring

from my pocket. "You could still marry me, I love you. Anna Groves, will you be my wife?"

She looked down at the one-karat diamond and then back into my eyes. "Eddie. I can't do that to you, it's unfair. This is my problem, not yours; I just have to figure out how to tell my parents." She sounded defeated as she spoke, then she stood leaving me kneeling on the ground, and started to walk back to my truck, "Can you please take me home?"

Standing I slipped the ring back into my pocket, walked back to my truck, opened the passenger door, and helped her in. Then I moved around to the driver's side and drove her home.

Before she could slip out again, I laid my hand on hers and said, "Anna, I love you. I have since you were fourteen. And I don't care whose baby that is. I still want you to be my wife, the baby is just a bonus." I knew I was pleading with her, but I half felt responsible.

She turned her head and looked at me, there was a sadness there I have never seen in her eyes, "I love you too, I always have. Eddie and that is why I can't marry you." Opening the door, she slipped out laying my jacket on the seat. She closed the door, and I watched her walk into her house closing the door.

I drove around for a couple of hours, finally stopping at a nearby bar. As I walked in, I saw people I had gone to school with some younger some older. Just as I stepped up and ordered a beer. A hand wrapped around my shoulders, "Well look who it is, fellas. Eddie Lambright. Our one and only hometown hero." It was Billy Yates; he was a year behind me in school, and an ass then, and from the sounds of it he has not grown up.

"Billy." I nodded and sipped at my beer, trying my best to ignore him.

Billy wasn't done though, "That Anna Groves sure is a beauty." He whispered to me, my eyes narrowing as I looked down at my beer. "She turned me down countless times in school because of you." I didn't answer, praying that he would stop, but I have known Billy since elementary school. If he had something spiteful to say, you could not stop him.

"A while back I heard you got out of the Marines. Figured you would come home sniffing around her again. But you didn't." He was giddy as he slapped my back again.

"So..." He dragged on, "I took another shot at her. Didn't like being turned down and all." His grin was just pure evil, and I have seen evil. "Finally, she gave it up, and lordy to my surprise, the bitch was still a virgin!" He leaned closer to me, "Knocked the bitch up I did, with just one shot." Sighing, "She sure was one tasty piece of ass, too bad you missed popping that one."

I looked calm as I stood away from the bar, then I turned

and landed a right hook straight in his face. The noise of his nose cracking as my fist landed vibrated around us, as blood splattered across his face and shirt. He sounded like a girl in a horror movie, his scream was so high-pitched. I was far from done, I wanted to kill him with my bare hands, but the bartender had other thoughts. Just like in an old western, he pulled a shotgun from under the counter, pointing it straight at me. "That's enough!" He barked. Looking up at the twin barrows pointed at my chest, I lowered my fist.

The cops arrived a few minutes later, and I spent the night in jail. Laying on the bunk, my mind was racing around what Billy had said. He was the father of Anna's baby. I closed my eyes; I should have come home for her as soon as I got out of the Marines. I kept thinking that she would not be in this mess if I had come back for her as soon as I got out of the Marines. Guilt riddled me, making me miserable.

An hour after sunup, my father was standing just out-side of my cell. "Son, let's go home." His low baritone voice rang out.

Ashamed, I stood up, looking him straight in the eyes, I said. "I'll pay you back the bail money when I get home."

"No need, no bail." My father was always a man of few words. "I spoke to the judge, and he dropped the charges." The side of his mouth quirked up in a smile, as we got into his truck, "We are ole fishin' buddies." He explained, then continued. "I would've loved to see you bunch that little prick.

Broke his nose, I heard." Nodding still grinning. "I'm proud of you son. Don't know what he did or said, but knowing those Yates, he deserved it." Then he looked serious, "Don't tell your mother I said that."

Shaking my head, "Not a word, dad." When we got home, I called Anna, but she refused to talk to me. I walked around my parents' house for two days depressed. Even to the point of talking to the local recruiter. In the end, I left to go home, I tried to call Anna a few more times but she continued to refuse to talk to me.

| **four** |

Anna

Looking down at the little stick that was going to determine my future. It was positive, I am pregnant, no denying it. This was the third test I took; they all could not be wrong. Thankfully my parents were out of town for the weekend, and I could hide the evidence before they got home. That and I had a couple of days to think of a way to break it to them.

In those weeks before I went out with Billy, Linda pressed me more and more about Eddie. "You mean to tell me that you are still a *virgin?*" She whispered the last since we were at work.

"Yes." I looked around to see if anyone was listening to us.

"Well, shit!" She laughed, "You must be the oldest one alive." Then she thought, "Now I am on a mission to get you laid."

I just rolled my eyes and walked away, each time we worked together, she would suggest a new man. Then finally she came around to Billy. "Hey what about that Billy Yates? You haven't said anything, but hasn't he asked you out about a million times?"

"Billy? I thought you were sweet on him?" I hedged; she was right he has asked me out a lot in the last couple of weeks.

"No," she laughed. "I figured out he wanted to go out with you when all he would do is ask me about you." She shrugged, "And he was not impressed with where I live."

Angry for her, "What is wrong with where you live?" I grumbled, but I knew the answer, Linda lived with her aunt in the trailer park, and all the Yates' considered anyone that lived there 'trailer trash'.

Seeing that I was upset, "Nothing. And he isn't my type anyways. Too stuck on himself." Then she grinned, "But we need to get you laid, and he seems like a good candidate."

Lowering my head, I thought, *I want more than just 'getting laid'.* But didn't say it out loud.

"You're not holding out for the hunk, are you? I thought you were getting over him."

I lowered my head, maybe I was holding out for Eddie, "No, Eddie is not even here." I said, and she harrumphed.

Two days later, Billy asked me out again, and I accepted. It was the worst night of my life. Instead of the nice dinner he promised, we went to a diner just out of town, then we drove to a secluded spot nearby, where we had sex. It wasn't making love by any description. Billy was crude, and in a hurry, lifting my skirt, and shoving himself into me over and over. I bit the inside of my lip to keep from crying out. When he was done, he looked down at himself them me and laughed! "A fucking virgin! Wait til I tell the guys!" When he pulled off the condom, looked pissed, "Fuck it broke!" Then he shrugged his shoulders and pulled up his pants, he drove me home, still laughing, stopping in front of my house, he turned and looked at me, "Thanks for the fuck!" And that was it, thankfully I was able to hold back the tears until I got to my room.

I was in shock, first, at the way he treated me, and then he said the condom had broken. I ran into the bathroom and took a shower, scrubbing myself and any trace of him off and out of me. Praying, and hoping that I would not get pregnant, surely it would not happen the first time. But as those three tests now laying on the counter prove, it could and did happen the first time.

Now I needed to tell Billy. Closing my eyes at the thought, I had not seen or spoken to him since that night a couple of months ago. Pulling out my phone I found his contact and sighed as his phone started to ring. "What?" was his greeting instead of a 'hello'.

"Billy, it's Anna." Whispering.

"I know who the fuck it is. Do you know what fuckin' time it is?" He grumbled.

"Yes, it's nearly two in the afternoon." Realizing I was getting off track. "I need to talk to you, Billy." Looking down at the pregnancy test a tear slipped from my eye.

"So, talk, since you woke me up."

"This may be better done in person."

"Just spill it, Anna, I don't have time for drama."

Taking a deep breath, I didn't want to meet him anyways. "I'm pregnant."

"So, what has that have to do with me?" There was a sneer in his voice.

"The baby is yours." I was trying not to cry while on the phone with him. But he was making it impossible.

"Prove it!" he hissed.

"What?" I could not believe what I was hearing.

"I said prove it." He hissed again.

"Billy," I was trying to be reasonable. "You know I was a virgin until that night."

"So, how do I know you have not been spreading your legs all over town since." Pure hatred was all I heard now. Gasping at what he was insinuating, "If it is mine, then just get rid of it, there is a place over in…" Not wanting to listen to the rest, I hung up. A few seconds later, a text came through from Billy with the name of the clinic and address. "Get rid of it, and leave me the fuck alone." That was all he said.

Tears fell from my eyes as I deleted the texts and blocked his number. Running my hand over my stomach, "It's just us, little one." Standing I gathered up the tests, and boxes they came in, putting them in a trash bag, not wanting my parents to find out just yet, I plan on taking the bag to the dumpsters in the back of the store when I worked tomorrow.

Then I checked my bank account, I had been saving to go to school. But now my plans have changed. There wasn't a lot there, and probably not enough to start a new life somewhere else, not with a baby on the way. Having an abortion was not an option for me. I just had to think of a way to tell my parents. This would break their hearts, but I was not worried about them kicking me out, just their disappointment.

| **five** |

Mr. Groves

Walking into the family room just after Anna and Eddie left. "Well, he has finally is going to pop the question!" I announced to my wife.

"Who dear?" My wife asked not looking up from her knitting project.

Sighing, "The Lambright boy." I said exasperated.

My wife looks up smiling, "Oh, yes. I spoke to his mother today, she said he was home for a few days." Then she thought, "Anna has been in love with him for so long, I am happy those two are finally coming together."

Snatching the remote control, I sat down and mindlessly flipped channels, waiting for Eddie to bring Anna home. He was a good boy, and I know he would ask me permission to marry her. Lost in thought, I heard the front door open and close, then Anna's footsteps on the stairs.

My wife and I both looked at the clock, and it was not all that late. Then there were the slight sounds of Anna's sobs floating down the stairs. "I wonder what happened?" My wife whispered.

Making a waving motion with my hand, "Go up and find out!" I whispered the demand.

She shook her head, "No, we need to leave her be," she whispered.

Pushing myself up from my favorite chair, "Then I will go." I harrumphed back.

At the touch of my wife's knitting needle to my arm, "No, leave her be." She retorted and amended, "Anna will tell me when she is ready."

Nodding and sitting back down, "Ok." I sighed.

But Anna didn't say a thing for a week when my wife came down dressed and looking to go out. "I am taking Anna to Dr. Franks," she announced.

Seeing the question in my eyes, "Anna has been ill these last couple of days. I am pretty sure I know the cause, but I want it confirmed." It was a matter-of-fact statement, and I knew when my wife was in this kind of mood not to argue.

A few hours later, Anna was back up in her room, and my wife was in the kitchen, folding and unfolding a kitchen towel that lay on the table in front of her. Tears were in her eyes when she looked up at me and uttered. "Anna is pregnant."

My eyes widened in shock, "I will kill that, Eddie Lambright!" Anger filled my voice.

Exasperated my wife's next words stopped me from going to go get my shotgun. "Eddie is not the father." Seeing that I was confused, she sighed saying, "I assume you know how a baby is made and how long it takes to be born?"

She was going somewhere with this, so I sat down. Still angry over my daughter being left pregnant, alone to fend for herself, replying, "Of course I do."

Nodding she continued, "Anna is about three months along. Eddie was not here then." Then there was a look I don't think I ever saw in my wife's eyes, one of pure hatred. "Billy Yates was who she went out with back then."

I could feel the heat rising to my face, furious. "What the hell?" Now I wanted my shotgun. "I will kill that little prick." Fury still raged in my voice as it grew louder.

"Hush! And calm down." My wife ordered. "You will do no such thing." She was looking at the towel and then calmly said. "I will not have my daughter and grandchild saddled with that no-good Yates boy."

Nodding in agreement, all the Yates were the scourge of the county. All the money in the world, but not one was worth a damn. "My poor little girl," I whispered.

Shaking her head, "She isn't dying, she is pregnant." Still in thought whispering, "We need a plan."

"What are you talking about now?" I asked.

Looking back to me, "Anna said she told Eddie about the baby, and he still proposed." She offered as an explanation. The timer on the oven went off, and she stood. "Let me think about this for a while." She said, "I am going to make Anna a tray then dinner will be ready in about an hour."

Later that evening, I was back in the family room, sitting in my favorite chair as my wife was in the kitchen. I knew the dishes had been done at least an hour ago, I helped her load the dishwasher. Finally getting back up, I walked in to find my wife again folding and unfolding that stupid dish towel.

Smiling she looked up at me, "Even though we know that Yates boy is the father, Anna is not going to admit it." She said then sighed, "So, we are going to pretend we do not know either."

"Why?" That was all I got out before she continued.

Then still smiling, "Do you think you could buster up that anger again towards Eddie?" There was a wild look in her eyes.

Still confused, "I guess. Why?"

She sighed, standing. "I found out the address where Eddie works." She was now wiping down the counters again, "Tomorrow you get all that bluster up, and take Anna there and demand that Eddie do the right thing and marry your daughter."

I resembled a wide mouth bass my mouth dropped open so wide, then I asked. "What makes you think he will as again?"

My wife just smiled, "I talked to his mother, and she said he was down in the dumps for the days following when he asked Anna." She shrugged, "Besides, Eddie has been in love with Anna since she was fourteen."

So, the next morning, I woke Anna and told her to pack a bag. We got in my truck, and I drove to where Eddie worked. I felt bad, Anna looked worn out by the time we got there.

| six |

Hunter

Looking out the window from the upstairs office down to the main floor of Renegades, "Have you noticed that Eddie has been down in the dumps since he got back from visiting his parents?" I uttered.

Conner looked up from the computer screen; "Yea, maybe I should talk to him?" he responded.

I knew what that meant. Conner was passing the buck to me. Shaking my head, I went down to the main floor, skirting my way to where Eddie was standing back between the dance floor and pool tables watching out for any trouble.

Renegades was crowded and the music was loud, so I whistled to him, and nodded my head toward the back doors. Once we were outside. "What's going on with you?" I asked.

"Sarg?" His eyes gave him away when he responded.

Exasperated I said, "Eddie since we got out of the Marines, you only call me Sarg when something is wrong." I crossed my arms.

Looking down to the ground, he was shuffling some loose gravel around with the tip of his boot. "I was thinking of maybe going back in the Marines," he hedged.

"When did this happen?" I asked worried, we all were affected by what we saw in Afghanistan. Eddie was the youngest of our platoon, we all watched out for him.

Looking out to nothing. "I went in to see the local recruiter when I was home," Eddie muttered.

Sensing that this was not about wanting to re-enlist back into the marines, there was more to it. I took my phone out of my pocket, I called Conner. "I am taking Eddie for a ride out to the pond," I said to Conner when he picked up.

Slapping Eddie on the shoulder I insisted, "Come on, let's go. I'll drive."

Eddie quirked a smile; "Will Abigail be there?" asked with a grin on his face.

Shaking my head, "Eddie you need to get over the crush you have on my wife." I mocked. When we turned onto the road that led out to my property, I answered, "No, she is at the hospital tonight." He nodded then I asked, "How was your visit home?"

Eddie was looking out the passenger window, "Nothing much to talk about," he uttered. When we got to my driveway, he saw the new no-trespassing sign that read; "Trespassers Beware – Cat is on Duty" I saw him smile.

"Abigail got that for Charlie. It seems she has adopted the damn cat," chuckling as I pulled up to the garage, and as we walked through to the house, I grabbed a couple of beers out of the refrigerator that I kept in the garage we headed out to the back porch. "Eddie, what's going on? And please do not tell me you are looking to re-enlist." I urged.

Taking a sip of his cold beer, "No, I am just a little down I guess." He uttered.

Concerned I asked, "Your parents, are they okay?"

Looking over to me; "Yes, they are good. Mom made you a couple of pecan pies." Grinning: "Sorry, I ate them on the drive back."

Shaking my head, "You owe me for that, I love your mom's pies." Leaning forward looking out to the pond. "Then what has got you so down in the dumps."

Taking a deep breath, he sighed, "Anna."

I understood now. "She's the girl you wanted to marry when she got a little older?' I asked. Eddie had shown us pictures of her, with her pets, and in her cap and gown when she graduated high school, he was so proud of her.

"Yes, when I went home, I was going to propose." He uttered, as he reached into his pocket, pulling out a diamond engagement ring.

Patting him on the shoulder, "I'm sorry Eddie, did she turn you down." I sympathized.

Shaking his head, "Not exactly, she is in the family way." He said in his slow southern drawl as he twirled the ring around on his pinky finger, "She only told me, her parents don't know."

I closed my eyes; "And you are not the father?"

Shaking his head, "No, and the guy who is, well let's just say he is not standing up to his responsibilities. He suggested she get an abortion." Taking a deep breath, he continued. "The night she told me I went to a nearby bar, he was there, and when he saw me started bragging about how he got into her pants before me." He shook his head even though I could see the anger in his eyes. "He called her a tasty piece of ass."

My eyes narrowed. "And?"

Eddie grinned and shrugged, "I decked him. Broke his

nose. I wanted to kill him." Lowering his head, "I spent the night in jail. My dad talked to the judge and got the charges dropped." He was seriously depressed, "If I had gone home and proposed as soon as I got out, she would not be in this mess."

Before I could say something, I heard the garage door open, and Abagail was pulling in. She got out and opened the back door to her SUV reaching in for Jackson in his car seat, she looked up and then down the driveway. "Just a minute, Eddie. Abagail is home." I stood and walked out to meet her and take our sleeping son from her carrying him to bed.

"Hunter, Conner was pulling up behind me and there was another truck I didn't recognize." She was whispering to not wake up Jackson.

I laid Jackson down in his crib, leaving Abagail to tuck him in. "Eddie is on the porch, ask him to come to the garage." I softened the order with a kiss. There was an instant flash of desire in her eyes, so I grabbed her up for another quick kiss. "Later, I promise."

Walking into the garage as Conner was talking to an older man, when a pretty young woman stepped out of the second truck, looking worn out. She looked familiar. Eddie walked up behind me; "Anna? What?"

The older man saw Eddie and bellowed; "You did this to

her, and you run away!" I heard Jackson start to cry. Shaking my head, I knew Abagail would be out here in a flash.

And as if on cue she was in the garage with her hands on her hips; "Who just woke up my son?" Conner, Eddie, and I all pointed to whom I assumed to be Anna's father.

Not catching on that he just infuriated my wife, he bellowed again, "Edward Lambright, are you just going to hide behind that man, or are you going to be a man, and stand up to your responsibilities."

He was striding towards Eddie, I moved to block him from going further, "I don't know your name, but this is MY home!" Furious, "YOU WILL apologize to my wife for waking our son, and YOU WILL calm the fuck down." I seethed between gritted teeth.

Stepping back three feet from me, he looked around my shoulder to Abigail; "I apologize ma'am for waking your little one." Then looking at me; "I am Mr. ….

Eddie spoke up; "Hunter, this is Mr. Groves, Anna's father." He stepped around me. "Anna, you don't look good."

Abagail picked up on that as well, walking over to her, "You need to come inside and lay down." She advised, putting her arm around the young woman's waist, she ushered her toward the door into the house. Her father stepped close to stop them until he saw that I had moved to protect my wife.

Crossing my arms; "Mr. Groves, my wife is a nurse, and she will take care of your daughter." Looking over at Conner, "Let's move this conversation to the porch." He nodded, grabbed four beers out of the refrigerator, and followed along.

Moments later we were all sitting looking out towards the pond, none of us saying anything yet when Abigail came out carrying a fussy Jackson, "You woke him, you rock him." Then she handed my son to Mr. Groves taking the beer out of his hand. Turning to walk back into the house, she winked at me.

Mr. Groves looked over to Conner and then me, "What do I do?" He asked befuddled by my wife's actions.

Smiling, "I suggest you start rocking him." Leaning back; "I never question my wife's orders; Mr. Groves and I suggest you don't either." I said with a grin on my face.

Eddie stood laying his beer down on a side table beside the earlier one he had barely touched and walked into the house, not saying a word.

| seven |

Anna

I was sitting on the bed in the room the nice woman brought me to. I needed to clear things up with my father. It took us twelve hours to drive here from home. Whenever I tried to explain he would stop me from speaking and grumble he would handle things. The worst was he would hardly look at me.

The drive didn't sit well with me and I wasn't feeling well, but I needed to help Eddie, he didn't deserve any of this. Just as I tried to get up the woman walked in, "I am Abigail. And you are Anna, right?" her voice was much sweeter now than when she came into the garage.

Nodding; "Yes ma'am." I tried to stand but got lightheaded and weak in my knees nearly falling over.

Gently Abigail helped me back down on the bed; "No, you

stay right there." She ordered and then asked. "How far along are you?".

My eyes widened. "How did you know?" I asked tears coming to my eyes, and my hands went to the small bulge on my stomach.

"I figured it out when your father's bellowing about responsibilities." She smiled then looked at my pale complexion, "When was the last time you ate anything decent?" She changed the subject.

Just then there was a light tap on the door; "Miss Abigail, may I see Anna?" It was Eddie, standing there looking worried as he glanced at me.

Opening the door, "Eddie. Yes, you stay with Anna, don't let her up. I am going to get her something to eat." Abigail said as she turned and left the room leaving the door cracked open.

I looked up at Eddie, "She is nice." I uttered, ashamed of my father's behavior.

Nodding, Eddie stepped close and knelt in front of me, looking into my eyes; "Anna, I tried to call you several times. What happened after I left?"

As he spoke, I looked down at my hands, "Momma,

noticed I was getting sick in the mornings." Shrugging: "She took me to see Dr. Franks."

Eddie nodded, then laid his hand on top of mine asking, "Did you tell them the baby was mine?"

Tears were streaming down my face, "No, they assumed. I am so sorry Eddie, I know I am a grown woman, but I just got scared. And I could not tell them about the real father."

"You mean Billy Yates?" He stated. Shaking his head when I opened and closed my mouth. Then he answered my un-spoken question, "I saw him at the bar that night." Then he pulled the diamond ring off his pinky finger and slipped it onto my left hand. "Well, if I am going to be a father, then you and I need to get married." I looked at him; "Anna Groves, I love you with all my heart will you marry me? And let me be the father to your baby?"

Shaking my head, "Eddie, I can't do this to you." I tried to get up again, "I will talk to daddy." I said a little stronger.

Putting his hand on my shoulder, "Yes, or no? Anna?" Eddie's voice was hard and unwavering.

I have known Eddie all my life, and I knew when he got a notion, he would not let it go. "Yes." I breathed out.

Abigail knocked, "I have some soup for Anna. Eddie, can you help her to the table?" Standing, with a big grin he swung

me up into his arms and carried me to the table. Kissing my
cheek as he sat me down.

| eight |

I sat with Anna as she ate and made sure that she finished all the soup that Abigail had warmed up for her, and the crackers too. When she was done, I carried her back into the bedroom, laid her on the bed, and covered her up. "You rest. Let me deal with your father." I ordered.

Going back out to the porch, Mr. Groves had a sleeping Jackson on his shoulder. "Mr. Groves." I whispered, "Anna has consented to be my wife."

Hunter looked up at me shocked, I knew he was going to say something. I just shook my head. He looked over to Conner.

Mr. Groves, Hunter, and Conner all stood at the same time. Hunter took his sleeping son from his arms. Mr. Groves was as happy as all get out. Shaking my hand; "Congratulations my boy. I knew you would do the right thing." He was whispering.

Smiling for his benefit, "Thank you, sir." He looked around for his daughter, "Anna is sleeping." I looked over to Hunter holding his son, "Hunter, would it be possible for Anna to sleep here for the night?"

Abigail was at the doorway, "Of course, she can stay." Then she took her sleeping son from her husband and back into the house.

Mr. Groves looked after Abigail as she disappeared through the patio doors, "Sir, you have a wonderful woman there." His voice was appreciative to Hunter, "I don't think Anna's momma has ever raised her voice at me the way your wife did." He was scratching his head puzzled. "Well, I guess I will find a place to stay for the night, and we can head home in the morning."

Not wanting Anna to have the chance to change her mind, I decided it was time to take charge of the situation. "No sir, Anna and I will be married here as soon as I can get the license in order. That is best." Looking up to Conner, I added. "Anna can stay at my apartment starting tomorrow, and I can bunk at Renegades if that is okay with you Conner." It wasn't a question, but he nodded anyways.

Mr. Groves nodded, "You may be right. Her momma

will be disappointed not to plan a big wedding, but ..." He trailed off.

Conner stood, "I will host the reception at Renegades when they have a date set." He was looking at me and I knew he wanted to say something to me, but he was not going to argue in front of Mr. Groves. Glancing back to my soon-to-be-father-in-law he added. "Now, Mr. Groves if you want to follow me back into town. I can show you a nice place to stay for the night." With that, they both headed towards the garage and out to the driveway, Conner was following and stopped and whispering to me, "Eddie, I saw that look you gave Hunter, you and I will be talking tomorrow."

Shaking my head; "Sorry, Conner. My mind is made up." I said standing firm in my decision.

Nodding Conner walked towards the garage behind Mr. Groves. "Hunter." He grumbled a silent order for Hunter to talk to me.

As Hunter walked them out, I heard him say, "I will talk to him."

I was back in my seat when Hunter came back to the porch. "Eddie, are you sure you know what you are doing?"

Even though I was nodding, I said, "No, but I know I love Anna more than anything, and I will love this baby as my own." Looking out to the pond. "And I will not send her home in disgrace." Standing I held out my hand to my long-time friend whom I considered a big brother; "Will you be my best man?"

Standing to shake my hand, "Sure, why the hell not." Hunter chuckled.

Abigail was standing in the doorway wiping a tear; "I just love weddings!" Then she gave me big hug, kissing my cheek, "You will make an excellent father."

Then looking over to her husband; "Now you have that promise to keep. Please take Eddie back to Renegades and get home as soon as you can."

Hunter's face widened with a mischievous grin; "YES Ma'am!" He said with a mock salute, He was enthusiastic to get me out of the house, nearly pushing me out to his truck in the driveway.

| nine |

Mr. Groves

As soon as I got checked into this little motel and closed the door to my room, I pulled out my cell phone and called home. "I don't know how you knew, but everything is working according to your plan," I said to my wife on the other end.

I could almost see the smile on her face, but she hiccupped a sob, replying. "I knew he would marry her. And he will love that baby as his."

Not as confident as my wife I asked, "Are you sure?"

Without a pause, "Eddie can't father children. He had scarlet fever as a child." She explained.

Not believing my ears, "How long have you known this?" I asked.

"Oh, years," she sighed. "I remembered after y'all left this morning." Then I could almost hear her thinking. When she said. "I will call the cater and the church tomorrow."

"Hold up a minute, not only are they getting married, but Eddie is insisting they get married here." I drawled. "And I agree. For Anna's sake." Before she could make an argument, "I don't want that Yates' boy making any trouble for my Anna."

With a sigh, "You are probably right." After a moment or two, "Where is Anna now?"

I told her the whole story about the drive here and Eddie's two friends. "I tell you. That one called Hunter is a big fella. And I was a little afraid for my life when I was bellowing at Eddie," I said.

My wife was laughing, "You're exaggerating," she hiccupped.

Smiling that I got my wife to laugh. "I am not!" I retorted. "And the one called Conner. Not a big talker that one, but I would not want to meet him in a dark alley if he was mad." When she finished laughing at my story, I explained. "Anna is sleeping at that Hunter's house for the night. She was worn out by the time we got here, and not looking good."

"You left her with strangers?" she fumed.

Sighing, "Hunter's wife is a nurse and is taking good care of her," explaining. "And I will go back out with Eddie tomorrow to take Anna to his apartment to stay until they get married." I finished. I heard a hitch of breath, "Don't get your feathers ruffled there. Eddie is going to be bunking at the bar he works at. Everything is on the up and up."

I heard my wife let out a sigh of relief, "Okay dear, get some sleep. I will call Anna in the morning. Or should I wait and let her call me, that is what I will do, she needs to call me with the big news." My wife was rambling on, and if I didn't cut her off now, she could go on for hours and hours.

"Night dear," I said and disconnected the phone. I was not even sure she heard me; *she is probably still prattling on.* I thought with a smile.

| ten |

Anna

The sun was peeking through the curtains as my eyes slowly opened, I wasn't in my room at home, but I felt rested. The events of yesterday came slowly to my mind. Then I raised my left hand, there just where Eddie placed it, was the most beautiful engagement ring. Tears streamed down, I was engaged to Eddie. I had dreamed about being his wife for years and years. But I still felt I was using him, and it wasn't fair to him. Slowly I sat up, morning sickness or what I would call all-day sickness had hit me full force. I could throw up at the drop of a hat. Thankfully I didn't feel the urge to run to the nearest toilet or trashcan.

When I felt like I would not fall on my face, if I stood, I slowly one foot at a time came up off the bed. I was still in the clothes I had worn to travel here with daddy. Then I saw my bag laying on a chair just near the bedroom door. Daddy left me here. But I was determined to straighten out this mess. I love Eddie with all my heart, but I could not make him marry me, just because I was pregnant with another man's child. *'No, I corrected in my mind. This was my child. Billy gave up his right when he told me to get rid of it.'*

The sound of little hands hitting the door, made me smile, then I heard Abigail whisper, "Jackson! No, Anna is still sleeping."

Calling out, "I am up." Abigail cracked the door open.

Peeking in, "I am so sorry did this little monster wake you up?" She said then frowned that I was standing up. "How are you feeling?" She asked with a worried look across her face.

Smiling, "Better than I look, judging from your expression." It was a joke, but just then a wave of nausea hit, and I covered my mouth.

Abigail quickly dashed across the hall to open a door to a bathroom, "In here!" she called out. I made it just in time, I heaved for a few minutes before I felt like a wet rag doll. Sweating, and shivering at the same time. I laid my forehead against the cool porcelain of the bathtub.

Abigail stepped into the bathroom, with a cool cloth that she handed me then flushed the toilet, closed the lid, and sat. "I am going to call Dr. Morrison, my OB, and have him prescribe something for your nausea." Then she looked up,

"Hunter," She called out, as she stood and walked out of the bathroom.

Her husband stepped in, without a word, and picked me up, carrying me back into the bedroom laying me gently down on the bed. "Go back to sleep, Abigail's orders." He said then shrugged his massive shoulders and winked at me. I wondered how in heaven's name was she able to keep her hands off him, or other women away from him. I rolled over and laid my hand on my stomach, and softly said to my baby sleeping inside. "You are giving me some trouble already." Then I smiled and did just as I was ordered, I fell back to sleep.

Not sure how much time had passed, Abigail knocked and walked in with a man. "Anna, this is Dr. Morrison." She stood back as the doctor looked into my eyes and listened to my heart. Then felt around my abdomen, "Abigail tells me you are getting sick."

Embarrassed, but thankful that I might get some relief from throwing up all the time. "Yes, sir. Quite often, morning, noon, and night." I whispered.

He nodded making mental notes then asked, "Are you allergic to any medications?" Shaking my head, no, I glanced up to see Eddie and my father standing back watching. Patting my hand, he said, pulling out a vial, and a needle, "Good. I am going to give you a shot of *Zofran* to help you with nausea, it will help immediately. Then I am going to write you a prescription for the same medication, that I want you to take three times a day about an hour before you eat or just when you get up."

Then he looked behind him and saw the audience, "I want her in my office tomorrow at two P.M. for a full examination," Without pausing he looked straight at Eddie, "I am sure you will make sure she is there."

Eddie nodded, concern on his face, "I will." He answered.

Abigail handed the doctor an opened packet and I could smell the rubbing alcohol, he rubbed the moist wipe against my upper arm, "Now just a little pinch." He uttered as the needle went into my arm. Patting my hand again, "Now you stay put for a few minutes before you try to get up." Then he stood and stepped toward the door, turning he looked at Abigail, saying "I would prefer that she stay in bed as much as she can for today, if possible."

Abigail nodded, "I am off this evening, Anna can stay here." Just like that the decision was taken out of my hands and Eddies too for that matter.

My father followed the doctor out of the room, rambling off questions, he knew my mother would ask as soon as she heard. And I was sure she would be the next phone call he would make. I would not be surprised if my mother was not here tomorrow to go to the doctor with me.

Eddie stepped in and closed the door, sitting on the side of the bed, "How are you feeling? Really." He asked worry all over his face.

Reaching out, "I am fine. Just this little one is giving me some trouble." I reassured him with a smile.

Gently he reached out his hand and placed it on my abdomen, whispering. "You have to stop giving your mama so much trouble." Then he did the most amazing thing, he bent over and kissed my stomach.

Tears fell from my eyes, "Oh, Eddie. Are you sure you could love my baby?" I asked, when he made that small gesture, I fell more in love with Eddie Lambright.

Reaching up he wiped my tears away, he answered "I am very sure." Then he softly kissed me. My stomach rumbled, "I think I need to feed your mama." He whispered to my stomach as it grumbled again.

Moving the covers back, I tried to swing my legs over off the side of the bed. "Not so fast, you heard the doctor. You are to stay in bed today." Eddie ordered stopping my movement.

Rolling my eyes, "He said to stay in bed as much as I could, not all day." I retorted back.

There was a knock on the door, it was my father. Nodding

to Eddie, "I am headed home to get your mother. We will be back tomorrow afternoon." Then looking at Eddie, "You will make sure she is taken care of and gets to the doctor."

Eddie nodded, "I will make sure, sir," he answered. Then he stood and shook my father's hand.

When Eddie finally permitted me to get up to eat, he sat with me the whole time, making sure that I didn't eat too fast, so I would not get sick, when I was finished. I sat in the living room and watched him play with little Jackson. He is a mini version of his father. After an hour, Eddie looked at me and stood, then picked me up, "You are falling asleep." Then he carried me to the guest room and tucked me in.

The sun was still up when his finger caressed my face. "Hi," I whispered sleepily.

Sitting beside me, he had a prescription bottle and a glass of water in his hand. "Take one and sit still for about thirty minutes, before you get up. He read off the bottle and then handed it to me.

After I took the medicine, he reached out and took my hand, "I am sorry." There was a sadness in his eyes as he whispered, when he saw the confused look on my face, "I should have proposed to you as soon as I got out of the Marines." He explained.

My head was shaking back and forth, "Eddie. No. This

is not your fault. I was not some naive teenager that didn't know what was going to happen." I was adamant, then I lowered my head, "I should have waited for you." I confessed as a tear slipped down my face.

His two fingers were under my chin and lifted my head so I could look at him, with a soft smile. "We both made mistakes, then." His lips brushed against mine.

Trying to smile, "I should have never listened to that Linda," now there was confusion on his face, "She was a girl I work with, new to town. Teased me relentlessly about still being a virgin at my age." His hand had moved from my chin to hold mine as he listened, "She saw how Billy was coming around and thought he was cute. Said I should just give it up and get it over with." Then I dropped my head again, "I hated myself for listening to her, then I found out about the baby." Continuing, I moved my other hand to rest on my stomach.

"Anna. Shh, please don't cry." He said wiping away my tears, "This baby is going to have two parents that love him and will protect him." He laid his hand on top of mine lacing his fingers through mine.

I looked up with a smile, "He?" I giggled, "You are so sure I am having a boy."

He stood and offered me his hand, "Of course. A strong healthy boy!"

Swinging my legs over to the side of the bed I stood, followed him to the kitchen, and sat as he fixed me some more soup and crackers. He ate with me, then announced as Hunter and Abigail came in, "I am headed to work." He kissed my forehead and then moved to my mouth before he pulled away and left.

| **eleven** |

Eddie

While Anna was sleeping, I drove to town and picked up her prescription. I needed to clear my head. I had listened to her tell me about the so-called friend that teased her into having sex with Billy Yates, I controlled my temper as she spoke. She blames herself for not waiting for me. And I have blamed myself, for not going and asking her to marry me right after I got out of the Marines.

At the time, my mind just was not straight, and I just could not ask for her to marry me. I needed to work on myself. Clear the demons from my head, I had seen and done so much that I was afraid that she would end up hating me if she knew. The nightmares still haunt me at night, but I am better. Conner and Hunter were in the same situation until they met their wives. Both have said that the love of their wives has pushed those nightmares away.

One night, I called my dad. I had to find out what was

wrong with me. Why could I not shake the uneasiness, the terrors that come in the night? He was in the service, maybe he could tell me. "Son, it is normal. I still have those god-awful nightmares some nights." Then he paused, and said, "I still have not told your mother of everything I saw and had to do in the service or our country. I am still afraid that she would hate me if she knew. But if it wasn't for your mother's love, I would not have survived those first years out of the service."

Maybe he, Conner, and Hunter were right, I needed Anna's love to help me. Then I thought about how I was going to tell Anna, that I was no saint either. Would she be upset if she knew that I had been with more women than I care to admit? Most of the time when we would get a small leave, Hunter and I would get drunk and find women who were more than willing to fuck until we dropped so we could forget just for the short time. That is how I ended up with the tattoo on my chest, Hunter took my drunk ass to a tattoo shop, and picked it out.

When I woke up the next morning, I saw the dragon on my chest. I cussed at Hunter and tried to wash it off in the shower. "It's permanent!" He called out, laughing as I scowled at him. I wanted to yell at him, but my head hurt just too much, that was the last time I let him get me that drunk, fearing that if I did, I would be covered head to toe in tattoos.

Not long after we started to make out plans to leave the Marines, getting drunk and fucking our way through woman after woman was not the answer to dealing with what we had witnessed. It was time to leave and never come back.

Finally, I got Anna's medication, I stopped by my apartment to grab some clean clothes. When I pulled up there standing by my door were Layla and Sophie. Conner and Dylan's wives. And little Caroline was jumping from one foot to the other.

Layla came up and hugged me, "Congratulations, Eddie." Then she turned and looked down at her daughter, "Eddie, Caroline needs to use your bathroom." I didn't hesitate and unlocked the door.

Sophie stepped up after Layla and Caroline disappeared through the door and down the hallway. Wrapping me in another hug, "I am so happy for you." She stepped in and looked around. "Not bad, but we will have this place cleaned up in no time." Then she proceeded to look in my bedroom, turning her head back out of the doorway, "I hope you have some clean sheets around here somewhere."

Abigail, Layla, and Sophie could conquer the world if they wanted. Layla and Caroline came out of the bathroom, and I smiled down at the little girl that was the image of her mother. *Maybe a little girl the image of Anna would not be so bad after all.* I thought to myself.

Layla was speaking to me, and I had not heard a thing lost in my fantasy of a daughter. "Excuse me, I didn't hear you."

"We are going to clean your apartment," she repeated. She looked around, "I am not saying you are a pig or anything."

At that precise moment, Sophie comes out of my bedroom door holding up a pair of my boxer briefs pinched between her fingers, "He's a pig," she called out. Then looking at me, "I hope you have a laundry hamper somewhere." She has her right eyebrow shot up so high it nearly disappears into her hairline.

Walking up to her I snatched my underwear from her hand and deposited them in the hamper located in my closet. Both Layla and Sophie start to laugh at my embarrassment. While I am in the bedroom, I grab the essentials for staying at Renegades for the next couple of days and deposit them in a bag. Coming back out to the living room, I hand Layla the spare key, and turn my head to Caroline as I head to the front door. "Caroline you're in charge!" Her excited laughter is contagious as I head to my truck.

| twelve |

Anna

The next day my parents arrived in time and my mother went with me to see Dr. Morrison. Eddie was insistent that he was there saying he was not going to miss any appointments, and that he was going to make sure that his child was healthy. I saw my mother lower her head as she smiled and nodded.

I liked Dr. Morrison; he was nice and didn't ask questions about me being pregnant before getting married. He started a chart on me and measured my stomach, we got to hear the baby's heartbeat, and Eddie just smiled and nodded. When we went back out to the reception area, I was making my next appointment when Eddie came up and handed the office manager his credit card. Then he stated, "By next month she will be on my insurance. Do you need that information now, or then?"

She smiled up at him, "Then will be fine." Then turning

her attention to me, "Dr. Morrison has ordered a sonogram for you next month." Then she handed me a piece of paper, "These are the instructions before your appointment."

Eddie and I thanked her, and we walked out. My mother was waiting for us, as my father pulled up in his truck. "We are going to the hotel." She stated, then added. "We'll come to pick you both up for dinner at about six." Giving Eddie a hard look, "I assume you know of a nice place for dinner."

He smiled answering, "One better. Miss Layla has invited all of us to her and Conner's for dinner this evening." When he picked me up for my doctor's appointment, he grabbed my bag as well. Then drove me over to his apartment,

As he opened the door, grinning he said, "It is small, but we will start looking for a bigger place as soon as we get married." Taking my bag into his bedroom, he laid it on the bed. Looking around, "Layla and Sophie cleaned it up for you." Shrugging his shoulders, "I guess it wasn't up to their standards." Then he opened a couple of drawers, "And I had them clean these out for your things." Smiling he stepped to me, and wrapped his arms around me, "Are you okay?" he asked.

Confused, he responded, "You look a little overwhelmed." And even though I had not said anything he was correct.

Sighing, "I am, I guess." I sat down on the corner of

the bed. "We never really even dated, now we are getting married."

He knelt in front of me, "I am pretty sure we know each other better than most engaged couples." Saying as he held my hand turning the engagement ring on my finger, "I have known you all your life." Then to prove his point, "I know you like to fish, but won't bait the hook. Your favorite color is that blue of the expensive jewelry store."

"Tiffany's" I offered.

"You had a poodle as a little girl that barked at me constantly. And you have been saving to go to school, but couldn't decide on what to major in."

"I still haven't." I reached out and caressed his face, "And you are allergic to poison ivy, and swell up like a balloon whenever you get near it. You hated that dog of mine, you love to fish, and always refused to bait my hook. And I missed you so much when you went away."

"I missed you too. But I wanted to give you time, you were still so young when I enlisted. It would not have been fair of me to ask you when there was a chance, I may not make it back." He turned my hand kissing the inside of my wrist. "See we probably know each other better than most engaged couples out there."

"You are probably right," I said. Looking at his mouth,

"Eddie, there is something else we have not done, even though we are getting married."

He stood up, and offered me his hands, I stood up and continued to look from his eyes to his mouth, as he lowered his head to mine, "Anna, I have waited so long for this." Then his mouth was on mine, warm and soft. One hand went around my waist, then his other combed into my hair, and gently he tilted my head the way he wanted. "Open up for me Anna." He whispered against my lips.

As he captured my mouth again, this time tracing the tip of his tongue over my lips, I did as he asked, opening slightly. Eddie was not in a hurry, slowly his tongue slid into my mouth and mingled with mine. A low moan escaped my throat and I tried to step closer to him. He tightened his hold, just as he deepened the kiss. No one has ever kissed me this way, waves of desire coursed through my veins like a fever I never wanted to recover from. My hands tugged at the back of his t-shirt, pulling it free from the waistband of his jeans.

Then I slid them under and caressed his back. He was just as hot as I felt. My eyes tightened as I thought *This is how my first time should have been.* Moaning not with desire but with the anguish that thought brought me. I pulled back, and tears fell from my closed eyes. Eddie had not let go of me but gently laid my head against his shoulder allowing me to sob. "Tell me," He said.

Sniffing, "You're perfect."

"Hardly," he chuckled. "What was the thought that made you sad?" asking about my tears.

"The way you were kissing me," giving him only a vague answer. His hands were rubbing up and down my back, "I thought it was how my first time should have been." Then I pulled back enough to look into his eyes. "No one has kissed me that way before."

"And no one ever will, Anna." He pushed me back to sit back on the bed, sitting beside me. Holding my hands, he was turning my engagement ring, "Anna, you don't ever have to tell me about Billy. But know, he is not a part of our lives."

I nodded and accepted what he said. Continuing, "The first time we make love, I swear to you, I will make you forget all about him."

Smiling, "Can we start now?" asked.

Looking over his shoulder to the clock with the bright red time flashing, "Maybe when I bring you home. We need to get ready to go to Connor's and Layla's for dinner."

He stood, and showed me the bathroom, and where the towels were then held my hand as he walked to the front door. "I will be back in an hour, to pick you up." Then he winked, "For our first date."

Rolling my eyes, "Totally chaperoned by my parents, your friends, and their wives."

Stepping close to me, "Only until I bring you home." With that, he kissed me quickly and left.

Locking the door, I was excited. This was going to be our first date, I wanted to look pretty. Hurrying into the bedroom I went through my bag and found the only dress I brought with me. Then as I showered, I hung it on the curtain rod so that the steam would smooth out the wrinkles.

Taking my time with my hair, and a small amount of make-up, I slipped the dress over my head. Just as I heard Eddie knock on the front door before unlocking it, I stepped into my shoes. Standing back as he walked in, his eyes started at my feet until he reached my face. Admittedly, I did the same to him, as I looked from his boots up his jeans which were nearly indecently tight, then to the navy shirt, buttoned down the front. It hugged his frame perfectly, and his sleeves were rolled up nearly to his elbows. When I reached his eyes, there was a grin on his face as if he caught me doing some-thing naughty.

I started to step towards him, holding up his hand to stop me, "Stay there."

Confused I looked down at my dress, then back at his face, "Is there something wrong?"

Shaking his head, "No, but just like that day I told you, I was being shipped out. I memorized the smell of your shampoo and the way you looked on that swing. Now, I am doing the same thing; I am committing the vision of you standing there to memory. You are so beautiful, Anna."

"So are you, Eddie," I smiled back at him. "Did you memorize what I smelled like?"

Eddie stepped up to me, "I did." Taking my hand, "That memory got me through some very rough times." When he looked at me, there was more than just sadness in his eyes.

Laying my other hand on his chest, "Will you tell me?"

A small smile played across his mouth that didn't reach his eyes, "Someday, maybe." Whispering, then he leaned down kissing me softly, "But if we stand here much longer, I am going to kiss you silly, then we will be late to meet your parents."

He was distracting me from the topic, and I realized that there may have been things he experienced in the Marines that he just would or could not talk to me about. So, I let the subject drop. Stepping an inch back, "Then we had better skedaddle." I smiled up at him. Stepping around, I picked up my handbag and slipped my medication into it. Eddie came behind me wrapping his hands around to lay on my tummy.

Nuzzling my neck, he kissed me right behind my ear, "I have not asked, is our little one still giving you trouble?"

Smiling because I loved that Eddie referred to the baby as 'ours', I laid my hands on top of his, "The medication is working, I'm not running to the nearest toilet anymore at the drop of a hat."

He kissed me again, and I felt him smile, "You like being kissed here." Then he did it again, lingering. When I moaned, he pulled back. "Anna Groves, you make me hard as a rock when you moan like that."

Turning in his arms, I pressed myself closer to him, and I could feel the bulge of his erection straining in his jeans against my stomach. "That's good to know." I went up on my tiptoes, and kissed him, pulling back I looked into his eyes, moving my hand up and around his neck, I pulled his head down to mine, then lightly traced the tip of my tongue over his mouth, "Eddie," it was a whispered plea.

He did exactly what I wanted, his arms tightened around me as his mouth covered mine, and when he pressed his tongue against my lips, I didn't hesitate to open my mouth. Shy at first, I let my tongue slip into his mouth, growling as he tightened his hold on me. Gaining courage, I let my tongue play with his. Eddie could not decide where he wanted his hands, they were in my hair, then down my back cupping my ass and pulling me closer to his erection.

Pushing back, I went for the buttons on his shirt, and just then someone knocked on the front door. The deep voice of my father called out, "Are you two coming out any time soon?"

I laid my head on Eddie's chest wanting to cry. "Can you make them go away?" I whispered, breathing heavily.

Eddie kissed the top of my head, "He's your father. What do you think?" But I noticed his breathing was just as heavy as mine. "Go fix your hair. I'll stall them." Placing his hands on my shoulders, he turned me toward the bathroom, as he walked to the front door.

"Mary was worried Anna may be sick again." My father called out, stepping through the front door, I could hear the chuckle in his voice.

I called out from the bathroom, "No, just finishing up my hair." Looking in the mirror, I just hoped my lips would go down before we got to Eddie's friends' home. They are all swollen from our kissing.

Eddie had my handbag in his hand when I walked out, taking my hand, he pulled me close whispering, "Nice save." Then we walked down to his truck. He helped me in and then walked around to the driver's side. Starting his truck, "I intend on finishing that conversation later when I bring you home, Miss Groves."

Smiling looking out the front window. "Of course, Mr. Lambright." I agreed.

| thirteen |

Anna has been smiling all evening; dinner was some sort of chicken; I couldn't remember really. My eyes never left Anna. I wanted to tell everyone to go to hell and sweep Anna up in my arms to take her home to bed.

"Get that idea out of your head." Hunter came up behind me saying.

"What?" My eyes not leaving Anna.

"What you are thinking about just now. Her parents are just a few feet away." He said, lifting his beer with a grin.

Turning my head, I saw Mr. and Mrs. Groves in conversation with Anna, Layla, and Sophie. Sighing, "That obvious?" I asked.

Smiling, "Probably only to me and Conner." After he swallowed down his beer, "What's the plans for the wedding?"

Anna had moved to my side as he asked. I wrapped my arm around her, "We haven't set the date yet. But as soon as Anna decides we can get our marriage license three days before."

She smiled up at my friend saying, "We had better make it sooner rather than later."

Hearing our conversation, Abigail and Layla swooped in along with Anna's mother. "Well, then we need to take you shopping tomorrow to find you a dress," Layla announced.

Then the three women ushered Anna off to make plans for their shopping trip and look at calendars. It was a couple of hours before I noticed that Anna was yawning into her hand. I moved to where they all were, seeing magazines of wedding ideas opened around them. Smiling, "I guess I just have to show up," laughing.

Anna's mother looked up, "Don't you worry, we will have plenty for you to do, Edward."

"Yes ma'am," I answered.

"Have you called your parents?" she continued to me.

Nodding, "I did, and they are excited." Leaning down close

to Anna, "Are you ready to go home?" I whispered in her ear. Nodding yes, I helped her to her feet, and we said our good-byes. Mr. and Mrs. Groves follow us out and drove behind me until they reached the hotel where they were staying.

Then I took Anna back to my apartment. Walking in through the front door, and as much as I wanted to stay. She was tired, so I turned to leave.

Reaching out she took my hand, "Eddie, can't we finish that conversation from earlier?"

I looked down to see her cheeks were flushed, and I could only see the desire in her eyes. Taking her hand, I led her into the bedroom and opened some drawers, taking out a pair of pajama bottoms and a Renegades t-shirt. "You get changed," I said pointing to the clothes I laid out, "And I will be back in a couple of minutes."

Then I left the room and stripped of my shirt, boots, and socks. A few minutes later I hear Anna call out. "Eddie."

She had opened the door, and I leaned against the frame, looking at her. She smiled, "Making memories again?"

Continued to look at her, "You have to be the most beautiful woman in the world."

She pulled at the t-shirt that reached nearly to her knees.

And she had to roll up my pajama pants several times so she could walk. She blushed. "Don't tease."

Pushing off the door frame, I stepped close to her, lifting her face as I lowered my head, "I wasn't teasing." I reached down and picked her up thankfully she had turned down the bed, and I gently laid her down.

Her hands wrapped around my neck, and as I laid her down, she pulled me to her. I knew what she wanted, what we both wanted. Covering her mouth with mine, she opened for my invasion. Anna's tongue was just as active as mine, her hands were on my chest, in my hair, and she tried to get them down the back of my pants.

Scooting down, she huffed out her disappointment she could no longer reach to slide her hands into the back of my jeans, but I ended that disappointment quickly enough when I pulled up the t-shirt revealing her two perfect breasts. I kissed one taut nipple as I cupped her other breast, then sucked the nipple in my mouth. She moaned with pleasure. I was hard already, but that sweet sound made my cock demand to be released from my jeans. "Eddie, that feels so good."

Not leaving her nipple I just turned my head slightly and smiled at her, before redirecting my attention and mouth to the other perfect nipple. Worshiping both breasts with my mouth and hands, I then slowly kissed my way down her stomach, gently kissing her stomach. Reaching for the waist-band of the pajama bottoms she lifted her hips as I stripped them down her legs. She still had on the most delicate pink lace panties. "What a pretty presentation!" I uttered, kissing along the top. She moved so I could remove them. "No, I want you to keep them on."

I came back up to lay beside her, "They are perfect against your white silky skin." I reached up and with the tip of my finger, I trailed around her face, softly running it down her jaw and neck. I knew where she was ticklish, and I avoided those spots. I wanted her excited, my eyes didn't leave my fingers as they traced around both of her breasts, then back to her nipples. "You are perfect," I said, her breathing shallow as she watched me.

"Eddie?" It was a moan of desire, and I looked at her. The tip of her tongue peeked out as she licked her lips, and I wanted to taste her.

Leaning down I captured her mouth with mine in a kiss that was demanding and filled with need. My cock was throbbing to get out of my jeans, but I was not going to rush Anna. This technically was our first date, and I had no intention of doing the same thing that she experienced with Billy. She is precious and deserved better from me. Thankfully my mind didn't linger long on those thoughts. When she ran her hands down my back to the waistband of my jeans again, I reached behind me and stopped her, "No, not tonight." I said, "Tonight is all for you."

She looked confused, completely not understanding my

meaning. But she would in just a few minutes. Capturing her mouth again, in just a span of a second our kiss turned ravenous and searching. Shifting my weight, I came up on top of her, pulling my mouth from hers, I moved down her body until I reached the top of those lace panties. Slipping my finger under the elastic, I ran it back and forth watching her face as her eyes dilated, and her breathing hitches. Leaning down I inhale, "You smell amazing, Anna." Then I moved my fingers between to run down along the leg, "You shave?" teasing.

Her eyes were wide, and all she could do is nod. I moved one leg over my shoulder as I pushed her other wide. Then my fingers found her, slick and wet. Her clit was a hard nub when I traced my finger around it, she nearly bucked off the bed. "Shh, Anna. You are going to love this, I promise."

Then slowly I crocked my finger around the delicate fabric and pulled it to the side revealing her pink pussy. I inhaled again, "I am going to kiss you here." Letting the tip of my tongue slide from her wet entrance to her clit. I growled, "Just as I thought."

"What?" Her voice was excited and nervous.

"You taste amazing!" Then I grinned, "Time for dessert."

I didn't explain further, I just covered her cunt with my mouth. Swirling my tongue around her clit, sucking it into my mouth over and over. Her hand came down to my head, and she was torn between pushing me away and holding me there. Her body decided for her, as she arched her back moaning with pleasure.

"Eddie. I can't think," she moaned.

Letting go of her clit with a pop, I looked up, "Then don't. Just feel." Instructing, then dove in for more.

She did as I said, and her nails dug into my scalp, pushing me further into her. I held her panties to the side with one hand bringing my other to insert a finger into her. Slowly I fucked her, hooking the tip so that I knew I was hitting that sensitive spot. Even though she was no longer a virgin, I was careful not to push too hard or fast. Gradually I quickened my pace, adding another finger.

She was panting hard, her body was as rigid and she was on the verge of an orgasm. "Cum for me, Anna," I whispered, she opened her eyes, looked down at me, then licked her lips. There was an uncertainty in her eyes. "I am here, let it happen."

Two more thrusts and she bucked, her cunt convulsing around my fingers. "Good girl," I praised, and then leaned down to lick up the cum flowing from her. "So much, and all for me." I cooed. She continued to convulse for a few minutes before I brought her back down from her ecstasy. Slowly I lowered her leg from my shoulder and moved to lay beside her, wrapping her up in my arms. Then I reached over and covered her.

Anna turned in my arms and snuggled against my chest. "What about you?" she asked. Her hand trailed down my stomach. Laying my hand on top of hers, "I told you. Tonight, was all about you."

She raised her head, and looked at me, "I never." Blushing, "No one has..."

A possessiveness came over me, "And no one but me ever will." I stretched up and sealed my claim with a long kiss.

When we came up for air, "Are you going to sleep in your jeans?" she was teasing me.

Gently, pushing her head down to my shoulder, "I've slept and a lot more clothes than this." Kissing the top of her head, "Go to sleep." I commanded but didn't need to, her breathing had already evened out.

My eyes opened and turning my head I looked at the time on the clock, it was five-thirty AM. Untangling Anna away from me, as gently as I could then sat up on the side of the bed, but not before kissing the top of her head. Moaning in her sleep she scooted over to where I just lay and buried her nose in my pillow. A soft smile played across her face. Making me wonder what she was dreaming about.

Taking a quick shower and getting dressed, I leaned over her and kissed her, whispering, "Anna, I'm leaving." Her hand came out from the covers, and she reached for me, "No go back to sleep, it's too early for you to get up."

One eye opened, "Then you should not be up either, come back to bed."

Kissing her temple, "You don't want your mother finding me here when they come to pick you up to go shopping." I reminded her.

She blushed, "No, I guess not," there was a definite tinge of disappointment in her voice.

Laying her medication on the side table, with a glass of water. "Here is your medication," still whispering, then I kissed her lips and turned to leave. I just hoped she didn't get sick without me there to take care of her.

Driving over to Renegades, I let myself in through the back doors, turning to relock them. Then I walked up to the main office intent on getting another couple of hours of sleep on the sofa in Conner's office.

Just as I closed my eyes, a text came over my phone, "You had better set that wedding date quick before her father finds out you are sleeping with her." Hunter, of course, has the cameras in and around the club signal going to monitors at his home.

Smiling, "Thanks, dad!" I texted back. Then I leaned back and closed my eyes. The scent of Anna as she came last night filled my head and I could hear her moans again. Another memory that I will keep forever.

| fourteen |

Anna

My mother arrived around ten AM and looked me in the eye. I am sure there was a blush on my face, but she just patted my hand and smiled. "I won't tell your father."

Now I was sure there was a blush, but I didn't deny or confirm her suspicions. We met Layla and Abigail for breakfast at a little dinner, then headed to a bridal shop. Their friend Sophie came in a few minutes later, "Sorry for running late, I was …" she stopped. "Oh, never mind it is only interesting to me." Then she wrapped me in a hug, "So you are the one that has captured Eddie."

I liked her immediately. Layla explained to the shop owner that I would need a dress on the rack, we didn't have time to order one. By the time she finished explaining, Eddie's mother came in the door. She had a garment bag hanging over her arm, "Maybe just some alterations."

She draped the bag over a chair, she unzipped it. "Mama? Your dress?" I turned to look at my mother through tears.

Tears streamed down her face as well, "I wanted you to have the choice if you wanted," shrugging, "I called Elizabeth last night before they left and told her where to find it."

Looking back and forth from my mother to her best friend, my soon-to-be mother-in-law, "Of course, I would love to wear it."

When I looked at Layla, Abigail, and Sophie, they were all dabbing tears from their eyes. Layla finally stepped up, "Then let's see you in it."

The store owner ushered me with my mother's wedding dress over her arm to a dressing room. It took some time, but I finally stepped out to the ohhhs and ahhhs of my new friends and mothers. Stepping up on a platform in front of mirrors on one side of me, and everyone else was seated behind me. It was cream-colored, the skirt was full, and the bodice was snug, well the clips in the back held it snug. "Alterations will have to be made. We have an excellent seamstress on site." The owner said.

My mother stood, "She'll need a veil. That stupid poodle of yours ate mine years ago." She crumbled.

The owner brought out several that I tried on before we all agreed on one that matched perfectly. Layla pulled a credit card from her purse, saying that it was her wedding gift to me. My mother held up her hand, "Now, Layla. I don't mean any disrespect, but her father would have a fit if I let you pay for Anna's veil or the alterations." Smiling, "She is our only child and I have been saving for this day nearly from the day she was born."

Layla put her card away, "I can understand that. I started saving for Caroline's wedding a year ago."

Looking around, "Where is Caroline?" I asked.

"I left her with her father. She's probably at Renegades running around like a wild child." Answering. "I do need to pick her up soon," uttering as she looked at the time on her phone.

"Why, don't we all go? That way Mrs. Groves and Mrs. Lambright can see where the reception is going to be."

It was agreed, and we all went to Renegades, as Layla predicted, once we were let in, Caroline was running in circles on the dance floor, to different children's music being played through the speakers. "Mama!" she squealed when we walked in, running with her hands up to her mother.

Layla picked her up kissing her cheeks, "Having fun with daddy?" The child nodded and pointed up to a large mirror-looking window on the second floor. Conner and Hunter came out of a door. Hunter swung his son up on his shoulders as soon as they cleared the doorway. Both Abigail and Layla greeted their husbands.

A moment later, Eddie came around through a back room and headed straight for me. Kissing me soundly, Caroline giggled at the sight. Then Eddie released me hugging and kissing his mother. "Mom," the love he had for his mother was evident on his face. Then he did the same to my mother. "Now what am I supposed to call you? Mrs. Groves does not just sound right." He grinned.

My mother blushed at the attention, "You can call me Mrs. Groves until you marry my daughter, then we will talk about it."

"Yes, ma'am," He grinned moving back to my side.

"Caroline?" I spoke to the little girl, her bright eyes looking over at me. "Would you like to be my flower girl at the wedding?" The little girl wiggled to get down, and when her feet hit the floor, she jumped up and down, "Yes! Yes, please." Then she turned to look at her mother, "Mama?"

Layla looked at me, "Of course, you can."

Jackson didn't seem too enthused with the conversation, that when Hunter brought him down from his shoulders, Jackson laid his head on his shoulder and fell asleep. "Caroline wore him out." He whispered patting his back.

Abigail patted her son's back, "Too bad, we were looking for dates for lunch." She grinned at her husband.

Rolling his eyes, he looked over to Conner, "Catch the hint."

Conner had picked up his daughter, "I did." Then he looked at his wife, "The diner okay?"

She nodded, and reached for her daughter, "We will meet you there. Don't keep us waiting." Then she looked over to Sophie, "Might as well call Dylan and have him meet us too."

Eddie walked over to the bar and pulled a bottle of water out of a tub of ice, bringing it back and handing it to me. "So, you can take your pill." He whispered.

By the time everyone converged on the diner it was packed. My father and Mr. Lambright included. The owners were thrilled by the business, and pulled tables close together, and brought out a highchair for Jackson and a booster for Caroline. The little girl didn't want to be left out of any conversation, and announced loudly, "I am getting married too! Mama said so!"

All heads turned to her, "You are the flower girl, not the bride." Her mother corrected.

"But I want to be the bride!" Tears welled up in her eyes.

Conner asked, "Who are you going to marry?" His eyes twinkled at his daughter.

She smiled brightly at her father, "You, of course. Daddy." She was exasperated that her father even asked such a silly question.

Conner nodded at her answer, and we all heard him, "Damn right!" he muttered under his breath.

Lunch was great, but Conner, Hunter, and Dylan split the bill and stood to leave. Dylan said he had a client coming in, and Conner and Hunter needed to get back to Renegades. Layla and Abigail took their children home, and Sophie too had to get back to work. That left Eddie and me with our respective parents.

"Why don't we go over to the church, and see when they have any available dates for the wedding?" Then he leaned close to my ear, "Not going to let you change your mind." His breath was warm. When I turned to look at him, he was looking at my mouth. I could feel my cheeks heat with the thoughts of what his mouth did to me last night. "Keep that thought in mind for later." He whispered again.

"Son," His father warned.

Eddie stood, "Yes, sir," he uttered helping me to my feet. But the grin was still plastered all over his face for everyone to see, as were my flushed cheeks.

The pastor was there when we arrived and asked several questions. Some of which I didn't know how to answer. "It is only going to be a family affair. Our respective parents…" He motioned to his parents in the back of the church, "And then a few friends," he finished.

Looking down at his calendar, "We had a cancellation for the Saturday after next." Eddie looked at me, and I nodded. Then he pulled out his phone and called Conner giving him the date.

"All set," he said smiling. Placing his hand on the small of my back. "Did you pick out a dress, today?" he asked. keeping the conversation light. His father was watching us carefully, or Eddie more so.

"Yes," I smiled and looked at my mother and Mrs. Lambright. Not saying more.

Eddie looked at the three of us, "Are you going to tell me about it?" He was suspicious.

"Nope," I walked around him, "It's a surprise." Then I called over my shoulder, "Just making sure you show up to see it."

The next couple of weeks passed quickly, and today was my wedding day. I asked Abigail to be my maid of honor. And little Jackson got to be the ring barrier, though he nearly had both rings in his mouth before he got down the aisle. Hunter moved to pick him up and held him until it was time to pass off the rings to us.

When I stepped through the doors with Daddy on my arm, my eyes locked on Eddie. Only once did I catch Eddie wiping away a tear. After my father lifted my hand to place in Eddies, I noticed that Daddy had tears in his eyes too. Eddie gave me two surprises that day, the first arrived in the morning. A petite diamond pendant necklace. And when I turned to face him, he looked at it and smiled. And then when Hunter handed him, my wedding band, it wasn't the same one we had picked out, that one was simple. The one he placed on my hand had diamonds all around it. When I looked at it, a tear slipped from my eye, it was so beautiful.

As soon as our vows were over and we were pronounced man and wife, Caroline moved to her father, and claimed "Now me, marry me!" Conner soundly kissed his daughter and moved out of the church with the rest of us.

The reception was catered by the diner, and after we all ate, I was dancing with Daddy, "Are you happy my girl?"

Looking up at his worried face, "Oh, yes daddy!" I didn't understand his worry.

Nodding and sniffing back a tear. "That Yates boy back home would have never made you happy, you know."

My head snapped up; "Daddy?"

Kissing my forehead, "I can count, missy. I know Eddie is not the daddy to your baby." Nodding at his admission; "Your mother figured it was that Yates boy that was sniffing around you a couple of months back." Smiling and looking around, "The whole lot of those Yates is good for nothing. All the money in town, and not one is worth a bean."

"Oh, Daddy!" Realizing what he was telling me, I pulled away from his arms and ran towards the restroom.

Eddie must have seen that I was upset and followed me. "Anna?" Yelling louder before entering "I am coming in."

I was standing at the sink looking in the mirror looking at myself. "Daddy knows!" My head lowered, "He knew before he brought me here, that you are not the father." Looking up at Eddie in the reflection, "He tricked you into marrying me."

"Tricked me? Anna, I asked you to marry me out at the lake that night, after you told me about the baby. I figured something was up that night when ya'll arrived when he was bellowing at me." Eddie turned me and pulled me into his arms. Tilting my face up to his; "Have you ever heard your father yell at someone the way he was hollering at me that night at Hunters?"

I shook my head no, "But…." I was going to protest.

Shaking his head, "But, nothing. Anna Lambright, you

are my wife now, and forever." Then he gave me a crooked grin, "I think we have danced with everyone, why don't we get out of here? I have another surprise for you." Then he leaned down and kissed me softly at first, then more demanding. Pulling back a bit. "Anna, is that any way to kiss your husband?"

Giggling and shaking my head, I wound my hands around his neck and leaned in. Eddie pulled me closer; I could feel his hard cock pressed against my stomach. He lowered his head, "Open up for me." And I did just that. Sweeping his tongue into my mouth.

Mindless of our surroundings as our tongues danced together, I heard a small voice; "YUCK! Mommy and daddy do that!"

Eddie pulled away from me, I started giggling, he looked over his shoulder, "Caroline, where is your momma?"

Layla came to a halt at the doorway, "OH! We are sorry!"

My face was hidden in Eddie's shoulder, I could not stop giggling. Eddie nodded; "Miss Layla, I should not be in here, we were...." Shaking his head, "Never mind."

Taking my hand, he led me out of the restroom, and out to the dance floor. "One dance and then we are leaving. Okay?"

Smiling up to him, "Okay."

| fifteen |

Eddie

Dylan helped me when I called him a few days ago, to get the name and phone number of the owner of the cabin he had taken Sophie some time ago. I thought it would be a nice romantic spot for Anna and me to start our married life.

The day before our wedding, I came out and stocked the kitchen with all her favorite foods. And made sure everything was ready.

As I pulled up in my truck, Anna was looking out the window. "You can't see much now with it being dark and all." I explained, "But there is a really pretty lake just around the bend. We can go tomorrow if you want."

"It's pretty," she looked at the cabin.

When I got her inside, I realized that she was nervous, and I had to admit I was too. I had waited ten years to marry

Anna. Even though we had explored each other some these last few weeks, she was mine now.

I walked over to the refrigerator and got out a bottle of sparkling cider, "How about a drink?" And I showed her the bottle.

Anna looked at the bottle and nodded. I could tell she didn't know what to say. Opening it up, I poured two glasses and handed her one. "To Us, Mrs. Lambright."

She laughed, "Whenever you call me that, I have to stop myself from looking around for your mother." She sipped the cider.

Taking the glass from her hand, I set them both down on the table, "You looked beautiful today, did I tell you that?"

She smiled, "Several times, but it is always nice to hear. And you.." She stepped closer, and laid her hands on my chest, "we're so handsome standing up at the front of the church."

"Only then?" I teased.

She grinned, "Fishin' for compliments?" Lowering her eyes to my mouth, slowly they made their way back to my eyes. "You are always handsome, sir." She fluttered her eye-lashes and spoke in a forced southern accent.

Pulling her closer, if that was at all possible, I laughed out loud. "Why, thank you, my dear, Anna." Giving my best Rhett Butler imitation. She giggled.

Lowering my head, I kissed her soft, and when her tongue darted out to my mouth, we deepened the kiss. Her hands were up under my suit jacket, trying her best to get it off my shoulders. Pulling back, "Let me." I stripped my jacket off and tossed it onto a nearby chair.

She turned her back to me, her hair was up, and she pointed to the delicate buttons on the top of her dress. "Can you undo those for me?"

Other than the five buttons that were holding the dress closed, her back was bare. I trailed my fingers down her back, then back up to the buttons, enjoying the goosebumps that formed. I hoped it was from anticipation because it was warm in the cabin. With each button I worked open I kissed her neck. She squirmed, "Be still, I don't want to tear your dress."

Once I had the last button open, I slipped her dress down her shoulders, "Your skin is so soft." She turned her head slightly smiling.

Then she whispered, "Can I change?"

Placing another kiss on her shoulder I pointed to her bag on top of the dresser, "Your mama gave me your bag yesterday."

She walked over and took a couple of items out, still holding her dress up to cover herself, then walked into the bathroom. While I waited, I pulled off my tie and unbuttoned the top couple of buttons on my shirt.

When she walked out, she was wearing a sheer nightie thing, I didn't even know what to call it. Turning in a circle; "Do you like it? Miss Abigail insisted. Said it was her wedding present to me."

All I could do is stare at her, "You are beautiful." And she was the most beautiful woman in the world to me. Anna was petite, so much so that she was teased when we were young.

Her hair was the color of mahogany; rich and deep, and curly. She had worn it up but now it fell past her shoulders curling around her generous breasts. Her eyes were the color of milk chocolate, with little golden flecks in the middle.

She walked up to me, laying her hands on my chest. "Eddie, I am sorry."

Looking down; "What for?" I asked moving closer to her, my hands itched to touch her everywhere.

A tear streamed down her cheek, "I should have waited for you."

Picking her up, I walked over to the couch and sat down

with her on my lap. "We talked about this before, it doesn't matter anymore. You are mine now." And I kissed the tear away from her cheek.

Placing her hand on my cheek, Anna looked me in the eyes, "And you are mine." Sealing her pledge with a tender kiss. I had to remember even though she was pregnant she was still young and somewhat inexperienced. But lust was boiling up in me, faster and faster.

Treading my fingers through her hair, tilting her head back so I could ravage her mouth. Anna didn't resist opening her mouth. She moaned in my mouth, it was the sweetest thing I ever heard, then she squirmed in my lap. My cock was about to rip a hole through my pants, and I was sure she could feel me under her bottom. Sliding my hand under the nightie she had on, her legs were smooth as silk. Reaching her ass I cupped a round mound and squeezed. "Anna, I want you, I know you can feel how hard I am." Her eyes were wide at my frankness. She nodded. "We are going to go as slow as you want. I am not some asshole that is going to fuck you and walk off." Nodding again, "I want you to want me too." I sat her beside me and stood.

She watched as I opened my shirt, shrugging it off and tossing it over to the arm of the couch. "You are beautiful too, Eddie."

Running my hand down my chest and abs, and her eyes followed my hand. I grinned when I saw her tongue dart out.

Kicking off my boots, I knelt in front of her. Taking her hand I placed it on my chest, guiding it down my abs. Her eyes darted from her hand to my face, I could see the arousal, and the gold flakes got darker. "I am your husband now; you can touch me anywhere you want."

Letting go of her hand, she continued to stroke my chest, coming to a tiny scar I had on my left side. "Where did you get this?"

Looking down at her hand, "Afghanistan. I will tell you about it another time." Leaning in I kissed her soft at first then with the hunger I felt and knew that was bubbling up in her. Trailing my fingers up her leg again, "You feel like silk." When I reached her hips I scooted her bottom to the edge of the cushions. Tugging on the nightie she had on I lifted it over her head and tossed it on top of my shirt. She was completely nude, perfect, and mine.

She tried to cover herself, pulling her hands away, "Don't hide from me. You are perfect." My cock was straining to get out of my pants, but I wanted to go slow for Anna. Reaching up I caressed her cheek, then trailed my fingers down her neck. When I got to her breast, I could tell she was a little larger, "Are you tender?"

I was cupping and weighing her breast in my hand. "A little. Ahh, Eddie, that feels good." I was rubbing the pad of my thumb over her nipple, then I leaned in and took it into my mouth.

She moaned as I sucked, Anna's hands were in my hair and running up and down my shoulders and arms. Releasing her nipple, I ran my tongue down between her breasts and further. The hair above her pussy was trimmed, but I wanted to taste all of her. Pushing her thighs open wider for me, I kissed the top of the hairs there. Darting my tongue, I flicked it over her clit. "Oh…!" She gasped at the delicate touch. Her nails were digging into my shoulders, and I dove into feast on her, sucking and licking her clit. Circling the damp opening with my finger, I slide it in, she is so wet and ready for me.

Wanting her to cum, I lift my head and look at her, "Anna? Can you cum for me, baby?" And I go back to pleasuring her. "You taste so good," I told her between laps. With a slow hand, I start to fuck her with my finger, making sure to gently rub that sensitive spot inside.

I had brought her to orgasm several times over the last couple of weeks. I knew how much she enjoys being pleasured, and I want her to cum. I am fucking her with my fingers faster; lapping up the juice that pouring from her cunt. Her hands have moved to my head and she is holding me there; "Eddie…. I'm going to cum!"

She was tensing, "Just let go, Anna. Cum for me." She leaned up as the spasms of her orgasm hit her.

"Eddie!" She moaned as her pussy convulsed around my finger. It was all I could do not to open my pants and thrust my cock deep into this delight. Slow and steady I brought her down, she was wide-eyed with shock at what just happened to her. "You know just what to do to me."

Standing up I lift her, instinctively she wrapped her legs around me. "You like me eating your pussy?" It was a question, her head was in the crook of my neck, and she nodded. I laid her on the bed, "Good because I loved eating you. And intend on doing that to you a lot. You taste so sweet." I had unzipped my pants and sucked them down kicking them to the side.

My swollen cock bobs, coming up between her legs. I take her hand and guide it to my cock. "Touch me." Anna looked down and wrapped her fingers around my cock, I watched as slowly at first she slide her hand to the base of my cock and back up to my swollen head. "You're so hard and hot."

Smiling, "That is what you do to me." Taking her hand away. "I don't want to cum in your hand." Then I positioned the head of my cock to her entrance. Pushing into her, "You are tight." I stopped and let her get used to me, before pushing further. Continuing pushing, then stopped until I was fully inside of her. "My God, Anna. You feel so good."

Her eyes never left my face as I entered her. "Eddie, this feels wonderful. Can you move please?"

My arms were braced on each side of her, I watched her

face as I pulled out some and pushed back in. She closed her eyes and moaned, "Again, please."

Leaning down I captured her mouth and a ravenous kiss, as thrust into her deep, again and again. I wasn't sure if Anna could cum again, "Anna, can you cum again?" As if just asking her I felt her body edging towards another orgasm. "That's it, baby, let go. Cum with me."

"Eddie! Hold me!" She was gripping my arms tight.

Nuzzling her neck, "I'm right here Anna!" The feel of her cunt pulsing around my cock, I threw back my head and groaned as I came deep inside of her.

Still braced on my arms, she relaxed her grip. Opening her eyes, I was smiling down at her. "Now you are truly mine." Rolling to the side I brought her up against me.

She was stroking my chest, loving the feel of her touch. She was now exploring my abs and going lower. Stopping her hand, "Anna, I know I told you that you could touch me anywhere you wanted. But if you don't stop, I am going to get hard again."

She jerked her hand away, looking up at me. "Oh, I'm sorry."

Taking her hand and placing it back on my chest, "Don't

be sorry. If you want to make love again, we can. I intend to. Just giving you a little break." Then I gave her a light kiss.

| sixteen |

Anna

Laying here awake for the last hour or so, I looked over to see that Eddie was still asleep. The sun was barely up, but enough light streamed in through the windows that I could see all of him. The sheet was low on his waist, and I could see the outline of his erection. My eyes trailed down his body, he was all muscle from his arms and shoulders down to the rolling hills of his abs. There was a tingling in my fingers to explore, but for the moment I stayed still and continued to admire him.

The memory of him that day on our front porch, with his hair cut so short, he was handsome then but now there thought still handsome he was more. We both had grown up in those years we have been apart. Smiling I slowly leaned up, his hair was a deep dark brown, nearly black, still short but longer than it had been ten years ago. He has a beard now short, and I can still feel the whiskers on me when he eats me. That memory had me wanting him to do it again.

Slowly I pulled the sheet down exposing his hard cock, looking up, his eyes were open, but he didn't say anything. I placed my hand on his chest, running my fingers around his nipples. He sucked in his breath, as they got hard. Scooting closer, I leaned over his chest and licked one then sucked it into my mouth. My hand trailed down his abdomen until I reached his cock. I wrapped my fingers around his cock, stroking him.

"Anna, do you know what you are doing to me?" He moaned. Slowly he pulled my hand away and rolled over taking me with him. Slowly he entered me, his eyes never leaving mine. He rolled his hips and as he would push forward. My body, arched up, and I wrapped my legs around his waist, taking him deeper.

The orgasm that was building even before I touched him, was strong, and I could feel his body was rigid as well. "Eddie," I moaned.

"I know baby. Together, okay." I let go, as I felt the pulsing of his orgasm inside me. When we both could breathe again, he rolled over to his back, bringing me with him, laying my head on his shoulder. "You have worn me out wife, and it is too early. Go back to sleep." My body was more than happy to oblige.

Finally waking up, I looked over to see Eddie was in the kitchen making coffee. I got up quickly and walked over to the couch and grabbed his shirt and put it on. "I can do that for you."

Turning he looked at me as I was rolling up his sleeves. Smiling, "You are my wife, not my cook." Coming over to me, he tilted my head up and looked into my eyes. "How do you feel this morning?"

Blushing, "I am fine, thank you for asking." With that said, in the next instance, I was dashing into the bathroom to throw up.

Eddie followed me and pulled my hair back and got a cold washcloth for my face and head. "Not so fine then?" He picked me up and put me back on the edge of the bed. "Stay still for a few minutes." Going back into the kitchen he came back with my medication and some crackers and apple juice. "Take your pill and nibble on those, slowly."

Sitting on the edge of the bed I nibbled on a cracker. He was sitting beside me, watching me so that I didn't eat too fast. Placing his large hand on my stomach, "You need to stop making your momma sick." There was a small flutter.

Looking up into his eyes, I smiled, "Eddie. Did you feel that?" I asked excitedly. Holding his hand to my stomach, we waited only a few minutes before the baby moved again. Tears were streaming down my face, and I could see them shining in his eyes. "The baby moved." We both said in awe.

After another few minutes, the movements stopped, "Eddie, last night, is it going to be like that always?"

Eddie smiled; "I certainly hope so."

"That many times in a night?" I asked with a blush.

Grinning at me, "Night or day, we can make love as often as you want."

Looking down at my hands, "And will I ...?"

"Cum?" Eddie was so upfront.

Frowning, "Yes," I whispered. "I just never knew it would be like that." Thinking for a moment. "Momma didn't say anything about it when she talked to me."

Shaking his head, he chuckled. "No, I would not imagine that she would. Nor would my mother for that matter."

Standing up, he held out his hand to me, "Now wife how about a real breakfast?" He helped me up and we made breakfast together.

"Anna, you can ask me anything you want to know about sex." Smiling at me blushing. "You came apart in my arms how many times last night? And now you are as red as rose at me just saying sex." Getting up he came around and kissed me hard. "If I have my way, we will be having a lot of sex, love." Sealing that promise with another kiss.

Smiling up at his grin. "Do I get a say in this?"

Nodding he got serious. "Of course."

Standing up, I ran my hands up his chest. "What is more than a lot?" He wrapped his hands around my waist, as I snuggled closer to him; "Can we now?"

Leaning down to my mouth, "Yes, ma'am!" Then Eddie picked me up and put laid me on the bed.

| seventeen |

Eddie

Anna and I spent three days at the cabin, making love and walking around the lake. It was not quite warm enough to go swimming, but I intended to take her back when it was. Both of our mothers wanted to go to the sonogram appointment that was coming up early this week, then they were headed back home. Each night after we made love, I would lay my hand on her stomach, with hers on top, waiting for the baby to flutter.

Back at work, I was looking out to the crowd that had gathered at Renegades. Lost in thought I didn't see Conner approach me. "What's on your mind?"

Smiling; "I need to tell Anna something. I probably should have told her before we got married."

Concerned; "Come up to my office."

Following him up; "What's going on?"

It was my turn to look out the big picture window; "Anna wants a big family."

Conner was leaning against his desk; "And you don't?"

Shaking my head, "I can't." Looking over my shoulder to him, "I had scarlet fever when I was a kid." Looking back down to the dance floor, "The doctor told my parents I would never have children."

"Eddie, I am sorry." Then thinking for a moment, "This is why you decided to marry Anna. Even though the baby she is carrying isn't yours."

Smiling and shaking my head; "No, I have loved Anna for years, when I went home, I was going to propose to her." Seeing the stirring of a fight I dashed out the door of the office whistling to the other bouncers.

That night when I got home, Anna was awake and waiting for me. Thinking she would be asleep; I was trying to be as quiet as possible. "What are you doing up?"

She smiled up at me. "Waiting on you. Are you bleeding?" I looked down at my shirt where there were a couple of spots of blood.

"Oh, that isn't mine" Taking off my shirt over my head.

Smiling at the way she was looking at me I stalked towards her, "Anna Lambright, is that desire in your eyes." She giggled and ran to the bedroom. "Now I have you cornered." I laughed as I went in and closed the door.

After I had worn her out, "Anna, I need to tell you something."

Hearing the worried tone in my voice, "Did I do something wrong?"

Laying her head back down on my shoulder, "No, Love." Sighing, "You know how you want a large family?"

Nodding; "Yes?"

Laying my hand on her tummy, "What if this is the only child we can have?" I was looking into her eyes; I was worried I would break her heart.

She reached up and stroked my beard. "I know."

"You know what?" I was concerned.

She was continuing to stroke my beard. "Your momma, she said she knew that the baby was not yours." A tear slipped from her eye. "She said you can't have children."

I rolled over leaning up over her; "You knew?" Shaking

my head, "But you keep saying you want a large family." I was confused.

Smiling; "Eddie, there are a lot of babies that need parents." Running her fingers down my chest, "But it is fun trying to make them."

Growling low in my throat; "Yes it most certainly is." And I proceeded to show her just how much fun it was.

Within a month we found a bigger apartment and moved. Anna was a little restless being at home all day long with nothing to do. But trying to find a job being nearly six months pregnant would have been nearly impossible.

With the help of Abigail and Layla, they decorated our apartment. Finding furniture at thrift stores that they all spent time refurbishing. Our house was warm and cozy, and I could see Anna throughout it. When I would walk through the door from work, snuggling up to her body, she was my anchor.

We were at another doctor's appointment; Anna was nearing her time to have the baby. Abigail and Layla hosted a baby shower for her, at Hunter's. Within the last week, both our parents came to help when the baby comes. Well, our mothers anyway, I figured our fathers would spend time fishing.

Her contractions started in the middle of the night, and I

happened to be at Renegades. All I heard was a loud whistle over the speaker system, then Conner's voice ringing out; "Eddie it is go time!"

Running through the crowd, I got home in time to see Anna coming out of the apartment with my mother's arm wrapped around her. "Thank god!"

Getting her into the truck, I made it to the hospital in record time. Once she was settled in her room, I found out that my little petite wife had the grip of a powerlifter, she was nearly breaking my hand, with each contraction.

Finally, just as the sun was rising, Derwood Edward Lambright was born. We named him after her father and me. His face was all scrunched up as I held him in my arms. "You look like my grandpa Benny. That is what I will call you." Leaning over I kissed my wife and laid our son on her chest.

Our mothers came in cooing at him. My mom hugged me, "Are you, happy son."

Looking down at her, "Mama, he is my son. One day we will tell him the truth, but he is all mine." Kissing her forehead, "Do you like your grandson?"

She patted my chest, "Yes, he is my grandson." She wiped a tear away.

Our parents stayed for two weeks after little Benny was

born, we had either one grandmother or the other at the apartment helping Anna and me with him. But as before all too soon, they went back home. My mother sent me a copy of Benny's birth announcement they had placed in the local paper, Anna had it framed.

She was the best mother I could imagine, taking care of Benny. And would run herself to exhaustion if I wouldn't step in and take him from her insisting that she takes a nap. We kept our parents up to date on all his milestones, and now at two months almost crawling. Anna would place him on his stomach, and he would squeal as he kicked his little legs and flapped his arms around.

I had taken over some more duties at Renegades and would go to work a little earlier on Wednesdays. Walking up to Conner's office, my phone rang. Looking at the screen it was an unfamiliar number, so I ignored it.

The number called again twice, then my father called me. "Dad."

"Son, there has been some trouble here." He said.

I sat on the sofa, "Is mom, okay?" I lowered my head dreading that he was going to tell me something terrible had happened to her.

"No, your mother is fine, and so am I," he assured me.

"The Groves?" closing my eyes, I had not noticed Conner and Hunter come in.

"We are just fine," I heard Mr. Groves' voice come through the receiver.

Sighing, a new voice ran out, "Edward this is Mr. Cardinal, your father's attorney."

Looking up, I put my phone on speaker, "Why are you both at the attorney's office?"

My father spoke up, "Billy Yates is dead."

Anger washed over me as soon as I heard his name, "What has that got to do with Anna and me? He isn't a part of our lives."

My father didn't respond to my angered statement, "When they found him, they found his phone."

"Yates, father found the message Billy sent to Anna telling her about the abortion clinic." It was Mr. Groves speaking.

Hunter's hand squeezed my shoulder, "What does all this mean, sirs?" he called out.

"Hunter? Thank goodness you are there." My father said.

"Yates senior is claiming that Benny is his blood and only heir now." The attorney's voice rang out.

"Is there more?" It was Conner's turn to ask.

"Unfortunately, yes. Yates senior is threatening to sue for custody," the attorney replied.

"Over my dead body! No one is taking our son!" I growled, Hunter squeezed my shoulder again, and out of the corner of my eye, I saw Conner pull his phone from his pocket and stepped out of the room.

"Son," my father warned. "Benny was born in Texas, not Mississippi." He continued.

"Edward, you need to talk to an attorney there." Mr. Groves said.

"Dylan is on the way," Conner announced coming back to the office. When we disconnected the call, "Eddie. Go home, to your family. Tell Anna, we will be there in an hour."

Nodding, I looked at my friends, "They will not take him." I muttered walking out.

| eighteen |

Anna

Dread filled me when I saw Eddies face as he walked in. He couldn't look at me, just walked over and scooped up Benny from his pack n' play I had set up in the living room. Not letting go of Benny he came over and told me about the call. Tears ran down my face when I looked at him holding Benny. I could not say anything, just shook my head. My hands shook as I reached up to run them over my baby's head and back. Eddie pulled me close to them and wrapped his arm around me. "They are not taking him." He whispered repeatedly to my head.

When there was a knock on the door, I jumped up. "It's the troops," Eddie said. Then went and opened the door. Abigail and Layla came in, surrounding me in their arms. Hunter had Jackson, and Caroline walked in with her doll, followed by Conner. I smiled, Eddie took Benny into his room, and I followed to lay him down for a nap. I heard whispers and a knock on the door, then Dylan and Sophie came in. Our little apartment was packed with all our friends.

When we came out, Dylan and Sophie both had set up their computers on our dining table, and Abigail and Layla were in the kitchen preparing something I couldn't concentrate on. Dylan stood and pulled out a chair, "Anna, come sit down before you fall down." I did as he said, and Eddie sat beside me, holding my hand.

Dylan smiled. "Anna, this is Texas. The Yates, money does not mean a thing here." I knew he was trying to reassure me. Then he continued. "First, in Texas, it is very hard to take a child from their mother, you would have to be proven an axe murder." Smiling he continued, "Now, I know I am asking a lot, but I need you to tell me everything that happened between you and this Billy Yates."

Embarrassed that everyone was around, but I told Dylan everything. "Do you still have the text?" Sophie asked.

"No, I deleted it immediately." I answered, "I'm sorry I guess I should have kept it." When she asked, I handed her my phone.

"No matter, I will find it." Then she started to type rapidly on her keyboard. In a minute, "Got it." Then she handed me back my phone. "Wow, I know he is dead, but what a piece of work he was." Dylan looked over to her screen and shook his head. Then he continued to speak to Eddie about the doctor's appointments he attended and who paid for them. Also who was at the hospital when I delivered Benny? Layla came in and laid several glasses of sweet tea on the table. Then patted me on the back as she went to sit with her husband.

After all the questions were asked, Sophie didn't stop typing on her computer and would smile every so often. Dylan said. "Okay. I think I have enough to make some calls. Looking at both Eddie and me. "One, your fathers gave us a head start by calling you. Two, they are right, Benny is a citizen of Texas, even though he is a minor. Three, Mr. Yates will have to get an attorney here in Texas to sue you for custody."

Then he looked over to his wife, "Finding anything we can use?"

"Bits and pieces, I will have the full puzzle of the Yates family in a day or two." She grinned.

Dylan smiled, and leaned over, and kissed her cheek, "Thank god you are on our side."

Abigail walked in with Benny in her arms, bringing him to me. "He needs his mama." Then she patted Eddie on the back before walking over to Hunter holding out her hand, looking between Conner and her husband, "I need the Renegades credit card, we ordered from the diner to feed everyone."

Conner shook his head and maneuvered in his seat to take his wallet out of his back pocket. Handing her the card.

Caroline had been playing with little Jackson on the floor, then got up and ran to her mother holding her nose, "He pooped." She pointed to the little boy with her free hand.

Abigail laughed, and scooped up her son, "Babies do that." Then looking over at me, "Can I use your changing table?"

Just like that, everything seemed normal, but it wasn't. I tightened my hold on Benny. After the food arrived and everyone ate, our friends filed out the door. Dylan and Sophie were the last to leave. Slapping Eddie on the back, "You need to come to the office tomorrow and sign a couple of things, both of you." Then eyeing me, "Anna, I would tell you not to worry, but I know that is useless. But please have a little faith in me."

Eddie had his arm around me, as I nodded, holding back the flood of tears I knew would come. Billy Yates was trying to ruin my life from the grave.

| nineteen |

Eddie

That night for the first time, we had Benny in bed with us until Anna fell asleep, then I put him in his pack n' play I brought into our room. Anna was restless even in her sleep and looked like it had been a week or more since she slept when she woke up. It didn't get any better over the weeks until our hearing with a judge. Dylan had persuaded the judge that we needed a private hearing for all those involved.

Our parents came in two days ago, and as much as they tried, neither of our mothers could get Anna to leave Benny for a moment to get some rest. Even taking him to the bathroom when she showered. Anna was terrified that he would disappear.

Sophie's mother came to watch him while we were at the hearing. Finally, it was our turn, we came in and sat at the table Dylan indicated to, our parents and friends behind us. Mr. and Mrs. Yates strutted in and sat at the table across from us. I could see the resemblance to Billy in his father's snarl, he thought his money could buy him our son. I just had to keep faith that Dylan knew what he was doing.

When the Judge came in everyone stood. I held Anna's hand she was ice cold and shaking like a leaf in the fall. Dylan stood and addressed the judge, then the Yates attorney did too.

The Yates' attorney called Anna to testify, "Ms. Groves."

Dylan stood up, "This is MRS. Lambright." He corrected, "Please address her accordingly."

The attorney scowled, but nodded his head, "Mrs. Lambright, you had unprotected sex with the Yates' son, to become pregnant. Is that not true?"

"No, that isn't true." She answered, "We used a condom." Then she looked up to the judge, "He said it broke, then laughed about it."

"It broke?" he hummed, "Convenient."

Dylan stood, "Is there a question to be asked? Or are you just trying to make my client look bad?"

Throwing a glare toward Dylan, the attorney turned back to Anna, "And when Billy turned you down after you found out you were pregnant. That is when you and your parents came up with this elaborate plan to trick Edward Lambright into marrying you?"

Anna finally changed from being fragile, to angry. "NO! When I told Billy about the baby, he told me to get rid of it. He even texted me the address to an abortion clinic." She sighed, "I was a virgin until that night."

"A virgin!" the attorney laughed, "At twenty-six?"

Anna looked him straight in the eye. "Yes, I was." Then she lifted her eyebrow as in a challenge.

The attorney squirmed a second. "Then the elaborate plan."

Dylan stood again, but before he could say anything, the judge held up his hand, "Ask a question council or move on."

The attorney waved his hand, "I don't have any more questions for her."

The judge looked him in the eye, "For whom? Councilor?"

Knowing when to give up, he sighed, "I don't have any further questions for Mrs. Lambright."

The judge softly at Anna, "You can sit back down now."

Then it was my turn, still intent on proving that Anna

and her parents had tricked me into marrying her, but I was calm and answered his questions.

Then the judge called for a lunch break, and we all left for an hour. Anna would not eat, but Sophie's mother brought Benny to see us. She hugged him close as I fed her.

| twenty |

Anna

I felt like a rag doll that had been left out in the rain by the time I crawled into bed. I sighed with relief again that the Yates were returning to Mississippi without our son. After we got back from lunch Dylan called me back to the stand asking me about the night with Billy and his reaction when I told him I was pregnant.

Even pulling the copy of the text message he sent to me, giving me the address to the abortion clinic. After he read it out loud, before handing it to the judge, "When you received this message did you not perceive it to mean that he wanted nothing to do with you or the baby you were carrying?"

"Yes," I answered.

Then coming back to the table he pulled another paper out, "I spoke in depth with a Child Protective Services agent, and she signed this affidavit stating that the text message from the younger Mr. Yates is the equivalent of a parent giving up their parental rights in the state of Texas.",

As he was handing the paper to the judge, the Yates attorney stood up, "That text message was sent in the state of Mississippi, not Texas." He tried to point out.

Dylan smiled, "A text message is an electronic message, and will stand up in any state, sir."

The judge nodded and took the paper, Dylan turned to me, "Now, Anna. The Yates' are trying to say that you tricked Eddie, or Edward into marrying you. Can you tell us what happened?

"Eddie, came home a day or so after I realized I was pregnant. He asked me to marry him even after I told him about the baby." Then I smiled at my husband, "Even though I loved him so much, I turned him down."

"Why?" Dylan asked.

A tear streamed down my face, "I didn't feel it was fair to him, to dump my problems at his feet."

After a few more questions he called Eddie up to the stand and asked him about his military service, his decision to marry me, and who paid for all the doctor visits and medical bills. Then he asked questions about Benny, how old he was now, and progressing. Eddie answered with pride as he talked about our son. After that Dylan called Mr. Yates to the stand.

After swearing in he sat, "I don't know why you would call me." He huffed.

Dylan ignored his outburst, "Mr. Yates you claim that little Benny is your ONLY blood heir, is that not true?"

"He is my only blood heir." He nodded, "And that whore stole him from my son." He grumbled and pointed to me. I laid my hand on Eddie's leg, I could feel the tension in his body at Mr. Yates calling me a name.

Dylan, "Now, Mr. Yates, that was not very nice, and you know for a fact that is not true." Sighing, he turned, and picked up a paper from the table, "I hired Sophie Burnes Investigations to do a little work for me." Turning back, he read, "I have not one but four children listed here you have fathered over the years, that are still alive and well, and much older than little Benny, that could and fully intend on claiming a piece of your estate." Then coming back to the table, he pulled out several more papers, "And each of the mothers of these children has signed affidavits as well swearing of your paternity. Of course, DNA tests will have to be performed at some point."

Mr. Yates looked over to his wife who was dabbing her eyes, "All lies."

"Two of the mothers provided me with letters you sent them telling them as well to get rid of the bastard child. As you put it, you even wrote them on company stationery, sir." Dylan handed the judge the paperwork.

"There is more to what Mrs. Burnes found out, you have been paying support on the other two of these children for years. So, again, I will ask. Is little Benny your only blood heir?"

Mr. Yates lowered his head in defeat. "No, there are others." All the bluster went out of him.

Dylan had one more piece of information, "Mrs. Burnes also found three children that your son also fathered that are alive. And you knew about them as well, and financials show you have been providing for them."

Their attorney was listening to something Mrs. Yates was saying, abruptly standing, "Your honor, we would like to withdraw this lawsuit."

Mr. Yates looked up at his wife, and she nodded glaring at him, "Yes, we want to drop it." He muttered.

The judge slammed his gavel down, and I jumped startled by the loud noise, "Dismissed."

Dylan put his hand out and told us to stay there until the Yates had left. "Don't want to have to bail you out of jail

Eddie." He grinned. "I saw that look you gave Mr. Yates when he called Anna, well no use in repeating it."

Conner offered to take everyone out to dinner to celebrate, but I felt the weight of the last few weeks of worrying and lack of sleep. Eddie looked at me, "Thanks, Conner. But I think I need to get Anna to bed."

Our mothers agreed, and even offered to take Benny for the night, "No!" I cried out.

Eddie thanked them and kissed each on the cheek, "She needs him near her for now." Then he got me to the truck and drove us home, when I walked in, I went straight to Benny's room picked up, and carried his little sleeping body to bed with me. Without even undressing I laid down and curled my baby up in my arms, falling to sleep. I never heard when Sophies' mother left, or when Eddie came in to take little Benny back to his crib. I only partially remember Eddie undressing me and sliding into bed with me pulling me to his chest. I slept from the early evening until morning through. Only when I heard Eddie speaking to Benny, "You need to let your momma sleep, buddy. She is all tuckered out worrying about you." He was whispering.

Smiling, I was just about to get up when Eddie came to our bedroom pulling the door and leaving it open just a crack. "Just in case she needs us. Okay. Now how about a bottle," I listened as the refrigerator opened and closed, and I heard him talking as he warmed the bottle for our son.

Falling back to sleep, I woke up about an hour later to Benny cooing, on Eddie's lap, when he spotted me, he smiled, "ma-ma," as he lifted his arms to me.

Tears fell as I sank onto the sofa with them, "Can you say da-da?" I pointed to Eddie.

Benny looked confused, "ma-ma"

Eddie turned his head to me, "That's what's important now."

I leaned down and kissed him, "You are his only daddy."

We dressed and I fed Benny his cereal, as Eddie made coffee and breakfast for us both. When we sat down to eat a knock came at the door. "It's probably our parents." Eddie got up to answer, but he was only partially correct, all our friends were with them.

All with a worried look at me. "I am fine, I just needed a little sleep." My mother took over feeding Benny, as Mrs. Lambright went into the kitchen and started cooking for everyone. Thankfully Hunter and Conner had several grocery bags in their hands because I wasn't sure I had enough food in the house to feed everyone.

Soon everyone was laughing, and talking all at once,

leaning over, I laid my head on Eddie's shoulder, "We are all one big family." I whisper.

Kissing my head, "One big rowdy family." He agreed.

Hunter called out. "Anna if you can tear yourself away from pretty boy there, we are hosting a cookout at our house this evening." He grinned wide at Eddie.

Abigail called out, "We are what?" And everyone laughed.

Eddie looked at Hunter, "Did you forget to ask the boss?"

Hunter shrugged his shoulders, "I will make it up to her, later." Then he grinned at his wife.

She promptly blushed and nodded in agreement for the cookout.

| twenty-one |

Eddie

Having my family was wonderful. Benny was nearing two, and Anna had decided to go to school. She was restless to do something other than just being at home with the baby. She had been fascinated with the phlebotomists that took blood when she was in the hospital. And watched them. So, she took classes at the local college during the day, and I worked at night. Now I tease her about being my little vampire.

Anna was up for a promotion at work, and she had mentioned missing her period but thought it was just her nerves. We both knew I could not get her pregnant, so we never considered using any type of protection. I loved the feel of being inside her bare, it never occurred to us that the doctors in our small rural area could be wrong.

Anna came home, looking worried, and shocked. Benny was bouncing up and down on my back playing horsey. I knew right away something was wrong when she sat down. "Eddie, can we talk?"

"What's wrong, did you get passed over for the promotion?" I asked.

Shaking her head, "I fainted today at work."

"What? Are you okay?" I was looking at her head to toe. Looking for any signs of injury, even felt her head for a fever.

Looking down at the positive results, "Eddie who told you that you could not have children?" I was holding her hand.

Shrugging his shoulders; "Doctor Franks told my parents, why?"

She handed me the pregnancy test. "He was wrong. I'm pregnant."

I looked from her face down at the paper. "I don't understand." Looking at the paper again, then looking back at her I grinned, "Well hell! I am going to be a father again!"

Benny jumped up on the sofa with us, I grabbed him before he could jump on Anna. "Benny, you have to be careful. Momma has a baby in her tummy." Then I kissed his cheek before putting him down.

Waddling over to Anna he lifted her shirt, "Where?"

I laid my hand on Anna's still flat stomach, "The baby is sleeping inside."

Benny looked up at us wide-eyed. Then put his little finger to his lips. "Shhh, a baby is sleeping."

Hugging our son, tears fell from Anna's eyes. "Yes, the baby is sleeping."

Wrapping my arms around Anna, "Happy?"

She nodded then shook her head. "Yes, about the baby. But now we have to use protection."

Grinning back at me, "Not until after the baby is born though." Exactly seven months to the day we found out she was pregnant; our daughter Lillian Kay Lambright was born.

The End

FROM K. L. STEPHENS

Dear Reader,

I hope you enjoyed Eddie and Anna's story as much as I did writing it. These characters came to life for me as I brought them to existence for your enjoyment.

If you loved this book, please leave me a review! I love hearing from my readers. Make sure you read Conner, Hunter, and Dylan's stories as well.

There is more coming this year, The Lycan Knights series is continuing, with Levi's story will be next. I cannot wait to introduce you to him further.

And a new series will be coming this spring, called The Princes of Arcadia. A spin-off of the Lycan Knights. I can't wait for you to meet them.

Keep watch for Levi's story to be released in early 2023.

Thanks for reading,
K. L. Stephens

ABOUT THE AUTHOR

K L Stephens is the author of paranormal and contemporary romances. Her works include The Lycan Knights series, and two novella series The Bennett's and Renegades Roadhouse Series. Her books have received multiple rave reviews from fans across the globe.

K. L. Stephens loves to take her readers into the worlds she creates as she writes, where she matched her many flawed heroes, to strong women that come to love them despite their shortcomings.

Residing in Southeast, Florida with her spoiled Cocker Spaniel and lazy cat. When she is not working you can usually find her cooking, in the garden of her one-acre home, or reading. Her reading interests are as diverse as her writing. From classic, or sweet romances to spicy paranormal shifters and vampires.

MORE FROM K. L. STEPHENS

The Lycan Knights Series
THE PREQUEL
LUCAS
GRAYSON
LEVI (Coming 2023)

The Princes of Arcadia Series
Book One Coming Spring 2023

Renegades Roadhouse Series
CONNER
HUNTER
DYLAN
EDDIE

The Bennett's
INHERITANCE OF LOVE
INFILTRATION FOR LOVE
INTENSITY TO LOVE
IMPERVIOUS TO LOVE
INSTRUMENT OF LOVE